GANNY KNITS A SPACESHIP

David Gerrold

Cover designed by Laura Givens

David Gerrold
Visit my website at https://www.gerrold.com/

This Printing: Aug 2019
Eric Flint's Ring of Fire Press

ebook ISBN-13 978-1-948818-32-2
Trade paperback ISBN-13 978-1-948818-33-9

OTHER TITLES BY
ERIC FLINT'S RING OF FIRE PRESS

GANNY KNITS A SPACESHIP

"Why do we need a spaceship?" asked Ganny. The question wasn't rhetorical.

Gampy grunted, sucked some coffee from a bulb, left it hanging in the air while he scratched his ear and rubbed his chin and did his whole performance of being thoughtful. "Because," he said. And folded his arms.

Ganny did that side-to-side head shake she always did, accompanied with an expression of bemusement that usually decoded as "If that's the only answer I'm going to get, then I get to live with it." If Ganny waited long enough, eventually Gampy would explain. But by that time, she'd usually figured it out herself. Either way, Ganny knew better than to push. Wise people, she said, respect each other's orbits.

She meant that people who live in space live differently than people who live on planets. I'm not talking about the micro-gravity and the sense of confinement and the recycling of air and water and protein, the exercise regimen, and all the implants and augments, like bone-sintering and radiation-nanos and white-blood infusions, and all the other stuff that dirtsiders think about. That's just mechanics. You live with it.

No, there's something else. Dirtsiders don't notice it immediately, but they notice it eventually. And they notice it a lot more intensely than starsiders do because starsiders don't notice it at all. Starsiders live the way we do because that's the way we live. But dirtsiders say there's an emotional distance, a privacy wall, a cocooning. They say it's because of the isolation and the close proximity and the lack of elsewhere to go. According to dirtsiders, people who live in space are all introverts, socially enclosed, and given to long disturbing periods of self-inflicted privacy. They see it as being shut down. I guess, by comparison with dirtside, maybe that's true.

I've never been dirtside so I have no personal experience of what they're talking about, but I do watch dirtsider videos from time to time and if that's a valid reflection of how they think, I really don't want that experience. They talk too much about nothing in particular. Like, "What did you have for dinner?" and "How was it?" and "How are you feeling?" Like all that stuff is important. I know how I'm feeling, it should be obvious to everyone around me how I'm feeling. Just look at my face, okay? Maybe it's just me, maybe I'm missing something. But from where I am, they look stupid, they talk everything to death like they're incapable of doing anything on their own. And even if they can do it on their own, they don't do it until they've talked it over with at least six people. All that chatter. What's it good for?

Ganny says it's about bonding. They bond differently dirtside. I don't see why that should make a difference, but apparently it does. Ganny should know. Both Ganny and Gampy were born dirtside. I asked them once if there actually was that big a reality gap and they both had to stop and think. Finally Gampy said, "Ayep." And after a bit, Ganny added, "There might be more to it than that." But that was as much as either of them said at the time. So I figured it was one of those things that you have to do for a while before you can understand it. But dirtside isn't something I want to do. Germs and insects and airborne contaminants? Yick. I guess some people can learn to live with it. And if you've never known anything else, then that's what you call normal. It just looks dirty to me.

But I do know some dirtsiders. We exchange almost every day. They don't seem to notice the soup they're swimming in, and I don't mean the air and water, I mean the cultural soup, the context. But we don't talk about that much. That's too much like school. Oh, that's another thing. Living on the whirligig, everything you learn in school is about survival. Dirtside, you learn all kinds of stuff that doesn't have much application for anything at all, let alone survival.

But James, my dirtside boyfriend asked—well that's what I called him, he was never a real in-the-flesh boyfriend, and that was before I broke up with him anyway—James once asked if it wasn't lonely out here, not having any real friends. I told him I have real friends. I have friends all over the ecliptic and a couple on the long ride. Okay, they're all web-friends, but I don't feel alone. How could I? Web-friends are the best kind because you go to them only when you feel like it. They can't bother you any hour of the night or day like they could if they were right next to you in meatspace.

Okay, so I don't chat in real-time, but so what? Chatting has a lousy signal-to-noise ratio. It's mostly pauses while each person thinks about what they really want to say and what they should say instead. It's easier and more efficient to think things out first and then text it all at once. And when you send it as an email, you not only get to rewrite it a couple times before you click on send, sometimes you can even snatch it back if you have to.

What I mean is that talking is useful, sure, if you're talking it out to yourself, or writing into a journal, because that's how you figure out what you really think, but that doesn't mean you have to inflict that whole linguistic journey of ratiocination on the nearest innocent bystander. Because if you do, then that implies an obligation on your part to listen to them verbalize at length as they work their way through their own fumbling thought processes. Long, boring, tiresome. It's only interesting if it's about you, and if it's about you it's almost always something you really didn't want to hear in the first place, like someone's projection of their personal narrative about you, which is almost always negative and comes with the corresponding implication that because you listened you are now obligated to change yourself. And that's just silly. If it's the other person's narrative, not yours, it's their responsibility to author it in a way that's useful to them. What someone else believes, even if it's about me, is none of my business. I'm not so self-involved that I need to care. There are more important things. The only way information like that is ever useful is when you get it from more than one person because then you're hearing a common perception, but even then it's still only a report on the effect you're having on others. You're only obligated if you choose to be obligated. And most of the time, I choose not to be. That's how it is. No, that's not how *I* think it is. That's how it really *is*. Ganny says I could out-stubborn a cat. I don't know, I've never met a cat. I can out-stubborn a mountain, if that means anything, but that's a different story. When I say something, I mean it, that's all.

Never mind. This is about Ganny and Gampy. Whenever Gampy said we should do something, we all knew it wasn't ever just a casual thought, but that he'd been thinking about it for a few days or weeks, goggling and thinking and probably even arguing with himself. Gampy never said anything unless he'd already decided it needed to be said.

And then, after he'd said it, he knew that Ganny and I and whoever else might be in earshot would go off on our own and ask ourselves why he'd said it and we'd do our own thinking and goggling and thinking some more and probably a lot of arguing with ourselves as well. By the time Gampy's thoughts had finished echoing in the heads of me and Ganny and anyone else around, most of what we would have said didn't need to be said at all. Which is fine, because after you've lived in space with the same people long enough, you know them so well that you know most of what they're going to say before they say it and you really don't need to hear it one more time, so you learn to keep your cake-hole shut unless it's something that actually needs to be said. Like "You oughta come back in now. Your O-mix is getting a little thin."

So when Gampy said it, he wasn't just saying it. He was inviting the rest of us to think about it. Me, Ganny, the blue-crew, and all three of IRMA's personality-units. The Blue Crew worked three to six months at a time, depending on orbits, personal and ecliptic, alternating with the Red Crew. Some came back, some didn't, but Ganny and Gampy had a team of mostly-regulars and we didn't see new faces all that often.

Sunday dinner we always ate in the wheel, where we had real pseudo-gravity and Ganny could cook the old-fashioned way. Usually we had chicken roast, because that was the tradition, but not always. Chicken was just the fastest-growing protein. And most cost-effective. Ganny was a budget-nazi. But we also had goose, duck, swan, ostrich, dodo, pigeon, rabbit, beaver, beef, horse, pork, goat, venison, elk, antelope, moose, mutton, lamb, buffalo, tuna, swordfish, salmon, shark, lobster, shrimp, sea turtle, clam, squid, snake, alligator, rhinoceros, dinosaur, or any of the hundred different hybrid-proteins Ganny was growing in the meat tanks. We also had synthetic sasquatch, bandersnatch, yeti, and tribble. If you can imagine it, someone has probably already gene-tailored it.

The thing about protein farming, you don't have to worry about flavor too much, because you can add whatever flavor you want long before you start slicing, but you do want to pay attention to muscling, fat content, marbling, and digestibility. All the pieces of the viability equations. And of course, how you exercise the collagen web determines the texture and chewability, which is even more important than flavor. When you get all that balanced, then you either leave it alone, because some people prefer the natural flavor of the meat, or you start adding flavor components, genes, enzymes, hormones, whatever, because other people like their meat pre-spiced—but to Ganny it's all about cost-effective protein design. So even before the tissue-starters go into the growth tanks, she's doing targeted gene-splicing and chromosome-braiding and designer-musculature. Starsiders are always looking for better ways to turn CHON into stuff that tastes good, so you have to keep a big library of resources on hand, because you never know when someone is going to invent another new culinary fad, like rhinoceros green burrito or fried buffalo sushi or mango horse fish. On the gig there's always something that needs harvesting and even though most of it was grown to order, it always worked out that there was enough left over for dinner, sandwiches, stews, and snacks. Ganny said it was quality control. She wouldn't sell anything she wouldn't eat herself. Mostly.

Being born on Earth, Ganny and Gampy still had a few dirtside prejudices. Ganny was adamant that she would never grow chimpanzee or any other kind of ape, whale, or dolphin. Also on the list were rat, mouse, squirrel, possum, bat, cat, dog, wolf, hyena, lion, tiger, eagle, vulture, and most other scavengers and predators. No monkeys or elephants either. She did keep all those stem-cells in vitro, in case someone else wanted to buy starters for their own farms, but she wouldn't grow them for our own consumption. She did give in once on whale and dolphin, just to see, but she wasn't happy with the amount of water it took to produce a kilo of flesh, even though the water really didn't go anywhere and we always reclaimed it, but she said the recycling overhead had to be figured in and she felt it was prohibitive. That was what she said anyway. But while she allowed some wiggle room there, she was an absolute wall when it came to chimpanzees and other major primates. "I'm not a cannibal," she said. "I won't eat my cousins. Not even metaphorically. Maybe some people will, I won't."

Sunday dinner—that was when we did talk to each other. We shared what was important, all the stuff that needed to be said face-to-face. And if nobody said anything, which happened sometimes, because we were all too busy doing the knife-and-fork thing, slicing and stuffing and chewing and swallowing, which was the best acknowledgment of Ganny's hard work we could give, a lot better than silly verbalizing like, "Mmm, this is good." Of course it's good. If it weren't, we wouldn't be eating it. But if nobody said anything at all, Gampy would start poking. "So, Starling," Gampy finally said to me, "What did you figure out this week?"

"Railroads," I said. "Highways. Trucks. Costs of shipping."

"Mm," he said around a mouthful of something designed to approximate dinosaur, it still tasted like chicken. He chewed for a bit, swallowed, and finally asked, "And…? "

"Well, um. If you own the tracks, you have a monopoly, you set your own prices. But if you don't own the tracks—the roads—then everybody gets to compete, and the market determines the cost of shipping. In the ecliptic, there are no tracks, only orbits. And everybody's got their own. So it's like roads. It's all about intersections. Convenient intersections."

Gampy looked to Ganny. "See? Told you she'd get it."

Ganny swallowed politely before answering. "Was there ever any doubt?"

Gampy looked back to me. "Go on."

"I know we like to say that everybody comes to Rick's, because sooner or later everybody has to come to a whirligig to slingshot into a new trajectory, but that isn't true anymore. Not since whatsisname invented the traction drive. Used to be, they'd come for a slingshot, but now they only come if they want to fill their freezers. And that's only locals now, and only when they need to resupply, and only if they don't have a farm of their own. In ten years, fifteen, everybody will have tractions. Even cargo pods. So whirligigs are like internal combustion engines. Very useful, but only until people invented something more efficient."

"Good," said Gampy. "You might have been a little too optimistic about how quickly everyone will switch to tractors, but I might be wrong too. The human factor is always a monkey wrench."

"What's a monkey wrench…?"

"It's where you raise Jewish monkeys."

"Never mind, I'll look it up later."

"I'm sure you will." Gampy stuffed another baby potato into his mouth and grinned. That was his answer to almost every question: "Look it up, I'm not going to do all the work here, you're the one who wants to know." Gampy said the only thing worse than not knowing how to swim in the data-sea was knowing how and never getting your feet wet for anything more than looking at people trading body fluids. I didn't understand that one until I was eight, not because I was slow but because orbital physics was a lot more interesting than looking at boys taking off their underwear. Why do they do that anyway? I mean, okay, it's cute enough, but after a while you have to ask, what's the point? They all sort of look alike. Are those things really that important?

"So, kiddo," Gampy poked again. "Is a spaceship cost-effective?"

"Yes and no. I mean, a traction drive isn't that hard to fabricate. We could even print a couple dozen ourselves. There's enough open-source matrices on the web, we'd only have to choose one, maybe adapt it for our needs, so it's mostly a problem of raw materials and energy. And we wouldn't have any problem fabbing new solar panels, three or four racks and probably a dozen new capacitor farms, so it's only a problem of raw materials and we can cannibalize most of that from the junkyard. I'm guessing we could do it in 24 months or less. Worst-case scenario is 48 months. If we double up on the fabbers, I bet we could cut the production time to 16 months."

Ganny looked annoyed. Gampy covered his smile with his napkin. "What's the no part, punkin?"

"The life support system. We don't have a hull. Unless you're planning to cannibalize modules from the whirligig. But you'd never do that because the gig has to maintain a viability score of 350 or more for a crew of 20 and you won't risk the numbers. I don't know how big a crew you're planning for the spaceship, but even a yacht needs a lot of hull space to be self-sufficient."

"Why do we need to build a self-sufficient ship?" Gampy asked.

I gave him the look. The one that says "Why are you even bothering to ask?" It almost worked. He still gave me the "Come on, answer the question" gesture with his hand.

I took a deep breath, my way of showing him how annoyed I was that I even had to explain. "Because," I said. And folded my arms.

Gampy laughed. Ganny smiled and said to him, "She's got you there."

Of course, that wasn't the end of the conversation. Conversations never really ended on the whirligig, they just spun around for a while, evolving, changing, recycling. Some of the conversations eventually flung off into space, forgotten. Others got winched in for closer examination and winched out again when they were no longer relevant. I expected this to be one of those kind of discussions, I should have known better. Gampy never wasted air. Gampy was famous for that.

Actually, Gampy was famous for a lot of things. He and Ganny were sort of like legends. As near as I could tell, everybody in the belt knew them, or at least knew *of* them.

The way most people know the story, Gampy built the first whirligig. He didn't, not any more than Henry Ford built the first car, but Gampy built the first one that worked well enough to be profitable. You can look it up. Gampy started the first pipeline. And like the railroads, the pipeline made it possible for people to expand outward to Mars, the belt, and the Jovian moons. And the Saturnalias as well (their name for it, not mine).

The pipeline isn't really a pipeline with tubes, although I'm sure a lot of dirtsiders think it is. Once, when Ganny was angry about something, she said, "Never underestimate the stupidity of dirtsiders in large groups, except when they're alone and have to do their own thinking." And even though I know that there some smart dirtsiders, Ganny says not to depend on it. Anyway, the way the pipeline works, cargo pods come up one of the beanstalks, Ecuador or Brazil or Kenya or mid-Pacific, and also from Mars and Luna too. The pods go all the way out to the ballast rock at the far end of the cable, unless they're carrying cargo or passengers that can't stand the gees, and then they go only as far as they can. At just the right moment, the pod lets go of the cable and like a stone released from the end of a sling, it goes hurtling off in whatever direction it was pointing when it let go. Most of the pods go to Luna and Mars. A lot go to the Jovian moons. And a lot go out to the Saturnalias, now that they're getting serious about colonizing. A few more go out into deep space, those are usually long-distance robot probes. The rest come out to the belt where we catch them with the whirligig.

The whirligig is a beanstalk without a planet attached. You get a length of cable and two rocks, a kilometer is a good length, but you can do it with less—or more if you want. It works on any scale. Gampy says you really want a minimum of three cables for redundant strength, but he eventually used six, which gave him room for expansion.

You start with a cable and a construction harness. Then you catch two rocks—that's the hard part because it involves wrassling a flying mountain, and that's a lot of delta-vee, but if you can catch the rocks, or better yet, break one big rock into two pieces, you're in business. You catch each rock in a big net. You loop one end of your cable around one rock, you loop the other end around the other rock. If you're smart, like Gampy, you use multiple cables, because no matter how well you plan, you never know what surprises will happen once stress is applied.

Once you've got your rocks securely netted and harnessed and attached to the ends of the cables, you give each rock a push, but in opposite directions, a small push at first, just enough to start them orbiting slowly around each other like a bolo. That's the hard part because big rocks usually have their own opinions about where they want to go. That's what I mean about out-stubborning a mountain. Which is why as soon as you've got them going, you want to get out of the way, because you've probably miscalculated and you're going to have to apply a lot of corrections. That's why you start out slowly at first.

This is the part they don't always tell you about in the engineering books. In theory there's no difference between theory and practice; in practice, there is. The physical universe is going to get sloppy and you have to adjust for it. Constantly. Then you start adding more push, more acceleration, until you get your bolo whirling at the rotation you need to catch and sling cargo pods. Keep making corrections until you don't have to anymore. Wait a few days until they stabilize, then wait a few days more to see if you've miscalculated again.

With all that centrifugal force on the rocks, you want to be certain that they've finished settling. Sometimes pieces decide to fly off, which is why you want to get above or below the local ecliptic, so you're not accidentally in the way. You want to make sure that the whole thing isn't going to suddenly fly apart before you make a commitment. (Gampy says the same thing applies to women too.) Sometimes the stress and strain of applied "space-gravity" destabilizes the inner structure of the rocks, causing them to crack or crumble or simply rearrange themselves in their harnesses, changing their center of gravity and the center of gravity on your bolo. When you're finally satisfied that the bolo is spinning safely, then you proceed. Then the construction harness crawls back and forth along the cable until it finds the exact center of gravity on the line. That's where you build your hub, usually a wheel so you can spin it for gee.

Okay, so now you've got pumps on both ends of your pipeline. We're at the top end—one of the top ends. The bottom end is the great big whirligig called the big blue marble. A top end is any whirligig near your intended destination, or at least on the way there. You can sling a lot of stuff back and forth between the two. The tricky part is catching the pods. There are a lot of different ways to do it. The easiest is to hang a big hook at the end of the catching line. The pod then puts out a big loop of cable, as much as a kilometer in diameter, if necessary. If you're really cautious, you also put a hook on the pod and the gig puts out a lasso as well. The velocity differences at match-up are fairly low, usually less than a few kph.

But despite all the course corrections all the way in, you only get one chance at threading the needle. And with cargo pods carrying as much as a half-billion plastic dollars' worth of cargo at a time, you just don't take chances. And if the pod is carrying passengers, you *really* do not want to let them go sailing off into space, especially if the chance of recovery is somewhere south of impossible. Gampy says that having to listen to desperate calls for help fading off into deep space can ruin your whole day.

Gampy's whirligig outsizes everything else in this part of the belt, ten degrees east and seven degrees west, so we catch all the fastest and heaviest traffic in this slice of the arc. Seventeen degrees. And that's a lot of arc. That's because Gampy had the far vision. That's what Ganny calls it. Far vision is being able to see past tomorrow. A long way past. The way Ganny tells it, Luna got too crowded for Gampy's taste, so he hiked all the way out to the belt with a big roll of cable on his back, picked out the two biggest rocks he could find, hitched 'em together, and started 'em spinning. Then he ordered more cable. By the time the big space exploration companies got out here, Gampy had a giant spinning spiderweb with eight ballast rocks and sixteen stabilizing engines. Cargo slingshots through here for delivery to the local group or slingshots back and forth between Earth and Jupiter, Earth and Saturn, and occasionally even Earth and Mars, depending on everybody's orbital positions. Work it out for yourself. When Mars and Earth are on opposite sides of the sun, it's faster to fling it to us and we fling it on. It's called a double-play. Tinkers to Evers to Chance. I had to look that one up. The allegory isn't exact, but Gampy's a history nut, always peppering his conversations with little nuggets for me to find and research. He does it on purpose. It's the game we've played for as long as I can remember. But no matter how sharp I get, he's still the bear, I'm still the cub.

When a pod gets out here, it doesn't have to slow down. It only has to arrive at the right speed and the right time so that it momentarily matches trajectory with one of the spinning arms as it comes around. There are a lot of different spinning arms, different lengths, different positions, so there's a little wiggle room on the final approach, but not much. And IRMA takes over control of the pod on its way in and manages the entire docking maneuver. (If the pod doesn't let IRMA take control, we don't catch it. No matter what's on board.)

After a pod latches on, after the hooks and loops catch, there's a few moments of load-balancing, because even with all the ballast rocks in place, the whirligig's center of gravity has shifted and we either have to pump some water around or winch some other pods in or out, or both. IRMA manages that.

Some pods we winch down to the hub—and that requires more load-balancing. Others, we just wait for the next convenient launch window and send them whirling off to their next destination. Gampy says it's a lot cheaper for the big money to pay us to catch and sling cargo pods than build their own whirligigs. Gampy says that's how he became one of the first trillionaires in the ecliptic. On paper, anyway.

At any given moment, Gampy had maybe 950 billion dollars' worth of cargo in transit outward and maybe another 125 billion in value headed back, depending on market value. But depending on where the pods were launched from, depending on whether or not they had to slingshot around something, the outbound journey could take as long as three years. Complicating the matter, pods could only be launched when there was an open catching window for them at whatever point in the future they were scheduled to arrive, so the computations could get tricky.

But belters can't wait three years for supplies, not even three weeks if it's air and water they need. So Gampy always bought a lot of stuff on margin against a slice of long-term earnings. What that meant was that technically Gampy owned the cargo until the recipient paid for it. Somewhere, in some dirtside bank, somebody would subtract a few zeroes from one account and add them to another. Out in the belt, nobody starves, nobody suffocates. That's not just the Starsider ethic, that was

Gampy's rule. "Out here, the equations are as warm as we can make them. Anybody doesn't like that way of business can go somewhere else." Except for the longest time there was nowhere else.

Gampy never turned anyone away. If he had it to give, he gave. Only once did he have a problem with one family of belters. They didn't pay their bills. Even with all the computerized projections and advisories they had available to them, they always knew better, until eventually they mismanaged themselves into a very ambitious bankruptcy, but they kept on anyway. Because Gampy kept resupplying them for a lot longer than he should have. Until finally, it became obvious they were never going to work their way out of their very deep hole. They wouldn't take any of the little jobs Gampy offered them because they still believed in the big score, the solid-gold asteroid. Those little jobs would have kept them going and Gampy could have recouped some of their debts. But no. They were too proud to take little jobs. So finally, one night, Gampy loaded them up with just enough fuel and almost enough food to get to Mars, and as soon as they were all asleep in their ship, he slung them off to Mars. They made it, but they were really hungry when they arrived. The way Ganny tells it, a lot of other belters started paying their bills on time Real Quickly after that.

Every so often, some dirtsider complains about the amount of product that comes out to the whirligigs, enough to supply a small town for a couple of years, enough to build two or three long-riders. "I thought they're supposed to be self-sufficient. Why are we still supporting them? That money should be spent on the poor—not on spoiled starsiders."

But they don't understand. The whirligig *has* to be a warehouse. Maybe it's the way they live, everything is too easy. If you can waddle down to the corner store and pick whatever you want off the shelf, you don't worry too much about how it got there or where it came from in the first place or what it took to get it there because the next day the shelf is full again. Dirtsiders don't have to think about where their next breath of air or drink of water is coming from, so they don't stop to think that the rest of us do. Everyone who lives starside.

But the ones who do understand, the ones on the bottom end of the pipeline, they're even worse. Because every so often, one of those cute little business-school graduates figures that he can boost his bottom line by raising prices on the belters. Charge a dollar more per cubic liter of oxygen, two bucks processing fee for clean water, decontamination surtax for every item loaded into a cargo pod, no problem. It adds up. What are the belters going to do? Take their business elsewhere? Where? Negotiate a new deal? With whom?

The last time Gampy got one of those "New Fee Schedule" messages he replied with a new fee schedule of his own. "Service fee for new software processing to prevent returning capsules from accidentally falling into the Pacific Ocean or onto a continental landmass." The service fee was considerable. Enough to offset all the surcharges and processing fees and surtaxes. That was a fun negotiation. It lasted for eleven and a half months. Until a few of the capsules started falling into the Pacific. Including one very expensive capsule with a lot of stuff they really didn't want to lose. Oops. My bad. I told you we needed to update the software. Then they paid attention. Gampy appointed himself the ad hoc negotiator for all the belters and refused to back down until three planetary authorities agreed to regulate cargo launch costs more honestly. Gampy even wrote in a clause guaranteeing a cost of living margin for all the cargo handlers on the ground as well as the ones in space, so that guaranteed popular support from the important people on both ends of the line. A lot of dirtsiders weren't very happy about it. They said words like arrogant and blackmail and terrorism and wanted to stop sending us supplies at all. Obviously, they didn't think that one all the way through.

It wasn't a great relationship, but it worked. Gampy said it was about power. If you have it, sometimes you have to use it—to remind people that you have it. Otherwise they'll think you don't have it. But the whirligigs were important, just too important to the economies of four worlds and a handful of lesser settlements. Nobody could afford to get into a prolonged fight. The alternative was to accelerate things the old-fashioned way, by boosting a lot of fuel into orbit and using half of it to accelerate and the other half to decelerate. And twice as much more if you expected to bring anything or anyone back, because you pay a fuel penalty to boost the mass of your fuel, too. So before the traction drive was invented, the whirligigs were the cheapest way to sling things around the system.

It took a while to get the big traction drives out of the labs, but even before the first tractor ships started shooting around the system, everybody knew that the role of the whirligigs would be changed. Probably diminished. To run a pipeline, you need a sling at both ends, but a tractor can go directly from point to point and usually a lot faster. Cargo doesn't care how long a trip takes, passengers do.

So there wasn't any question why Gampy wanted a spaceship. It was the only way to stay competitive. Or we accept a reduced role in the economy of the belt.

Over the next few weeks, Gampy had us all working on the question of life support modules. Not just me and Ganny, but folks on the Blue Team as well. They were the real crew and he said their input was the most important, because they were the guys who had to make it all work. How big a module would we need? Could we afford to construct one? Or would we have to buy a hull from the Martian Electric Boat Company? What would our requirements be? How big a crew would we carry? And what about passengers? Will our payload include cash-carrying customers? How many? And what level of service will we provide?

The problem with that equation was that every time you added a warm body, you also had to expand the life-support systems to accommodate. Above a certain point—twelve is the magic number—there's a certain economy that kicks in. But when you start adding passengers, you also have to add stewards, at least one for every twelve bodies. It adds up.

There's a lot to think about in spaceship design. No matter how good all your software might be, you still have to make hard decisions about how far you want to go, how much you want to carry, who and how many you want to bring along, how you're going to keep everyone alive and comfortable and productive, and most important, how you intend to pay for it all. The irony of ship design is that there's a corresponding relationship between size and comfort and profitability. The more comfort you want, the bigger the ship has to be. The bigger it gets, the more people and cargo you can carry. The more you carry, the more profit you make. So the ultimate question is how big a ship can you afford to build? It's all about the life support module. The traction drive doesn't care. It's null-N, non-Newtonian.

So you can build a starter ship for five and later on add a second ring of cargo pods and maybe a couple passenger payload systems and you only have to add one or two or three traction cores to your basic unit. If you've designed for expansion.

So Gampy's real question wasn't about whether or not we should build a spaceship. It was about what kind of spaceship we were going to build. And that meant he wanted us to think about what we were going to do with it after we built it. Where do we want to go? And what are we going to do when we get there? And after that, then what?

We spent a lot of time on that question. We needed a keel—that was the easy part. But how long? We needed traction drives. But how many? We were already fabbing the fabbers that would let us fab the drives. We needed a ring to hold cargo and supply pods. But we still hadn't decided on the life-support modules. How big? How many people are we schlepping? That was why Gampy started the discussion in the first place. He'd probably figured most of it out for himself, but he wanted to see if the rest of us would come to the same conclusions. It took us a while, but we did.

The most cost-effective way to complete the ship was to buy a hull from the Martian Electric Boat company. It wasn't the cheapest solution, but it was the fastest. It would save us at least 8 months of construction and testing, and that would get us to the return-on-investment point that much sooner. MEBC was popping out certified hulls two a month, whether they had buyers or not, it was cheaper to keep the assembly lines running, but they never seemed to have an overstock problem, they sold everything they produced. Besides MEBC had over a hundred years of quality control, their hulls had already logged several quadrillion kilometers without a fatality, while we'd be starting from scratch, learning as we went and probably making a lot of mistakes along the way. But, as Gampy pointed out, if we did build the hull ourselves, we'd know every inch of it intimately. Maintenance and repairs would be a lot easier. And faster. Because we'd have a much more personal relationship with vehicle integrity.

Of course I shared all of this with my journal. I wanted to share it with my bf James, but Gampy said not a good idea. "Never share family business. Never share personal information. The person you share it with doesn't share your investment, doesn't share your commitment, and might not even care very much what happens to you. You can't know what he will do with the information. Don't take risks you don't have to."

"But James says he wants to come out here and work for us when he graduates. He can hitch a ride on a tramp. He's even willing to indenture. A standard seven-year contract."

Gampy didn't answer immediately. We were walking the centrifuge, we did it at least an hour a day, it was our best time for talking. But now he sat me down at the green bench, the one at the 60-degree mark. I think it was more because he was out of breath than because he wanted to be serious. "Starling," he said. "I need to talk to you in grownup now, so you

18

need to listen in grownup. This Sawyer boy might be a credible person. I think he is. Ganny thinks he is. Ganny looked over his emails, yours too. And he seems credible."

"You read my emails?"

"Yes, no. IRMA reads your emails, for your protection. She only flags for red-codes. Doesn't flag very often, so Ganny and I don't have to invade your privacy. But sometimes we check anyway. Shh. Let me explain why. Lots of suspicious people dirtside. Lots of fearful people dirtside. They live in fantasyland. Afraid we'll drop rocks on them. They watch us through telescopes. Everything we do, they see. They write, they speculate, they make things up. They get stupid. Living dirtside does that to you. Makes it easy to stop thinking. Dirtside, people can afford luxuries like stupid and crazy and not caring. Dirtside you can walk around wrapped in belief and ignorance and unconsciousness. But starside, no. The universe has an instant response to stupid. Vacuum is the fastest teacher. You're only entitled to one fatal mistake. No first warning, no second chances. So choose your death carefully, kidlet, you'll be stuck with it forever. And forever is long time, especially on the back end. Remind yourself of that. Say it every day. Like praying, but much more useful."

Gampy saw my impatient nod, I'd heard all this before, many times. He put his hand on my shoulder, his fingers felt frail. "Yes, munchkin. You know all that. But I want you to hear it again and again and again, because I want it written on your heart. Up here, this is the next step in human evolution. No, not spacelings or cyborgs, something more than that. It's about who we have to become in *here*, inside our souls. We're learning how to be conscious, awake, aware—truly *sentient*. That's what's important."

Gampy didn't usually talk this much, or this intensely, and I could see it was an effort for him, but Gampy only said what absolutely *needed* to be said, so I waited while he regathered his thoughts. "This is what I want you to know—dirtsiders don't trust us. Because dirtsiders don't trust anyone. Because they don't trust themselves." He made an annoyed gesture and I could tell he was thinking about someone in particular or a whole group of someones. "And they think everybody else thinks the same way—and anyone who doesn't is stupid. So everybody is either an enemy—or prey. That's why they watch us. A lot. To see if we're a threat or if they can take advantage of us. It's not just optical scopes, Starling, it's everything. They use data-scopes and web-agents and spybots. They want to know who arrives, who leaves. What we buy, what we sell. What we upload, what we download. Everything. The joke is—we have no secrets. Our business is open book. We are transparent. That's why they think we have secrets. They say no evidence of secrets is evidence of deeper secrets. Crazy dirtsiders only see what they want to see, only see what they already believe. They wouldn't see it if they didn't believe it. Remember that. Loonies and Martians not so bad. They have space-legs. But earthlings…? Too much dirt in their veins."

"But what does all this have to do with James?"

"Yes, James. Nothing, everything. Just be careful." Seeing my puzzled look, he took another deep breath. Labored. He had already used up a two-month quota of words and now he might have to borrow against next year as well. He patted my hand. "James seems like a credible boy. I hope he is. But because dirtsiders don't trust us, we can't trust dirtsiders. Not with important stuff. You understand?"

"Not all dirtsiders," I insisted. "Some are okay. Aren't they? You and Ganny were dirt-born. That has to prove something."

"Yes. But we were smart enough to leave. Some dirtsiders are smart. Some might even be trustworthy. But how do you tell? That's the big question. You figure that out, you're smarter than Ganny."

"Smarter than Ganny?"

His face crinkled impishly. "In all my life, I only outsmarted her once."

"You did? When?"

"When she asked me to marry her, I said yes. I don't think she expected that. Don't tell her I told you."

"Promise." I promised.

"Pinky promise?"

"Pinky promise."

Of course, like every conversation with Gampy, it kept me processing for a week. I finally went back and reread a lot of my old conversations with James. How we met, what we talked about. Everything. I didn't see it. I didn't see what Gampy saw.

So I kept looking.

James first howdied me three years ago. Nothing much, just a "Hey." I said "Backatcha." And that was most of what we said to each other for a long time. Non-communicative communications. "Agreed." "Yeppers." "Me too." Stuff like that. Somewhere in there, I decided we were simpatico. But looking back on the messages now, I couldn't find a lot of places where he actually said something on his own. Mostly he was restating my thoughts back to me. But so what? I did that a lot too. Whenever I saw something that I agreed with. So there wasn't anything out of the ordinary about that.

Then later, after a few months, he did tell me a little bit about himself. He was the oldest of three brothers. They lived in a container house in Baja, far enough south they could see the Ecuador beanstalk through a good telescope. His goal was to ride it up to the top. Someday. I asked him what a container house was, he explained that cargo comes in on shipping containers, it's too expensive to ship them back empty, so people buy a few, stack them, add plumbing and insulation, power panels and air-conditioning, and move right in. If you do it right, you can put together a pretty nice house. Resistant to earthquakes and hurricanes. Put it on stilts and it's flood proof. Fairly fire-resistant too. According to James. He sent me pictures. So I sent him a picture of me in the centrifuge, standing by the peach tree.

The peach tree confused him. He accused me of lying about living in space. I had to explain to him about Ganny's gardens and send him a different picture, taken from another angle, that showed just how small the garden was and how the hills in the background were really just a display on the inside bulkhead. I sent another picture of me and the peach tree with the background changing every two seconds, just to prove it. He apologized, of course, but....

So I ran the whole thing through IRMA, asking for a six-level transactional analysis with focused emphasis on semiotic dynamics. I'd never done that with a friend before, I'd always believed I was smart enough to judge for myself, but maybe Gampy saw something I'd missed. He wouldn't have said anything unless it absolutely needed to be said.

IRMA said that the peach tree transaction put me on the defensive and that affected subsequent transactions. Additionally, the information transfer ratio was three to one. I gave James three times as much information about my life as he gave me about his. He asked a lot deeper questions too. IRMA said his trust level was moderate, which was probably as good as you could ever get on the web, but she also annotated that sophisticated chatterbots could generate trust-levels that measured moderate to high because they were designed to do that. Even so, chatterbots were still limited in their responses in some specifically targeted domains of human interaction and that was how you could test them.

IRMA also said that some of my messages had been a little too candid, edging into the yellow area. Obviously, my physical safety was not at risk. But as an information channel, I had moderately compromised the integrity of the data-bubble. Even the alternate photo of the peach tree was suspect because it revealed that Ganny's farm was inside a reconfigured Xinhua-Mercedes cargo pod. But anyone with access to a Hubble-6 eye or better could see that from Martian orbit on close approach, and there were already plenty of photos on the web anyway. But IRMA was a skeptic. Naturally suspicious. Not paranoid like a LENNIE, but if an intelligence engine could raise an eyebrow, IRMA would have one permanently arched.

But okay, so Gampy's point was that James might be credible, but he might not be either. Hard to say. If dirtsiders really were as Machiavellian as Gampy believed then it wouldn't be beyond them to create a sock-puppet specifically to make friends with a lonely teenage girl in the asteroid belt, win her trust, and pump her for data about her grandparents' whirligig. Social phishing. IRMA reported that a preliminary goggle of his backstory checked out, but she had no way of testing if that data was seeded, salted, or homemade. Satellite views showed whole neighborhoods of container houses lining the highway from Cabo to La Paz. Street view of James' address showed an old blue Prius parked in front, with a rebuilt solar on the roof trickle-charging the battery. Whoever owned it, they were lucky if they were getting 125mpg out of that thing. With combustible at $545 plastic dollars per liter, it wasn't something you drove every day to work or shopping or errands. Maybe it was a project-car, or some old-timer's fancy, or I dunno. A relic of times past? Maybe dirtsiders didn't feel rich unless they owned a car, even if they couldn't drive it. Or maybe dirtsiders just didn't know better. Or maybe they didn't care. Gampy said that because most dirtsiders never got into space, not even riding the beanstalk up to One-Hour, they had no idea how small the marble really was, so they dropped trash everywhere. That's why they built mommy-bots—so they'd have someone to pick up after them. Stupid. It's cheaper to not drop trash in the first place.

There was more.

At first I didn't know who to be angry at. James for pumping me. Or Gampy for making me distrust James. Or myself—for not being smarter. Gampy once said we're never angry at anyone else. We're only angry at ourselves for not knowing better, for stumbling into the mess in the first place. For being played. Well, yes. I could see that.

I didn't answer any of James' messages for two days while I sulked. Plus we were six hours away because Earth was on the other side of the sun and everything had to relay around the belt, bounce off Mars, ricochet off Luna, and then down to the mudball, and besides it was September so the hurricanes were probably outpacing the sandstorms, which meant communications might be uneven for awhile, and even if not, email wouldn't be at the top of their immediate priorities, so James wouldn't be looking for a quick reply anyway and might not even notice if I was sulking, so that gave me time to think.

I could call him a big fat liar, but what if he wasn't? Then I could be losing one of my best-friends-forever. I could ask him to prove himself, but that would be almost as bad. If he was for real, I'd still be hurting the friendship, and if he wasn't for real then he'd know he'd been found out. And then I'd have to start worrying about all my other friends too. And any new friends I might make, because they might be sock-puppies too.

But this is why Gampy told me what he told me. So I would think about it. And what I finally figured out was this. If James Sawyer was playing me, then I would play him back. Oh, I wouldn't let him know I knew. I'd keep on going exactly the same, as if nothing had changed and everything was still like it always was. Only now, knowing what I knew, I'd be a lot more skeptical of everything he wrote and a lot more cautious about everything I wrote. And I'd test him, a little at a time, to see if he was a chatterbot or a sock-puppy or just a space-struck nerd. A space-struck nerd would be okay. That's what I thought he was from the beginning—a tall geeky-looking, boney-elbowed, gangly, big-nosed, near-sighted, horse-faced, freckly, redheaded goof with an incredibly beautiful smile, despite the buck teeth, and a terrific sense of humor. Unless he was a synthesized image, because there was always that possibility, too. Everybody had at least a half-dozen avatars for social-surfing. And if he wasn't for real, I was going to kill him. Even if it meant going down to the mudball in person. How dare he mess with my head like that? Well I could mess right back.

So I wrote to him and asked if he was all right because I hadn't heard from him in two days and the satellite view showed hurricanes all over Cabo and how weird it must be to have to think about weather all the time but please write me back asap because I'm worried about you. Okay?

Then I got back to work on Gampy's spaceship. Gampy said to think big, think outrageous. Imagine everything you think should be in the most perfect spaceship you can think of. Then he added, "You can have anything you want, but you can't have everything you want, so start out thinking of everything and then decide what you want most."

At first, I started out thinking I'd like a bigger personal cabin. But then I had to laugh at myself because personals are always high on the list for dirtsiders. A starsider always thinks of the crew first, what makes the community space better for everyone. So I started thinking about a garden-lounge, a bigger recreation area, and a more luxurious galley—things that felt both luxurious and comfortable. Expansive but homey too. I was afraid to want too much because I knew that we had to be practical. I didn't need anyone to tell me that.

James finally answered my email. He said the hurricane had been pretty bad and his parents' house had been shifted off its foundations and one of the containers had been yanked loose from its moorings and fell down and dented, and they weren't sure the insurance would cover the cost of repair or replacement or reassembly, and his little brother broke his leg when a table fell on him, but other than that, nobody was badly hurt. I didn't know how to answer him, except to say, "Mother Nature is a bitch. Father Time is an asshole."

But I knew that wasn't enough. How do you give sympathy to someone who chooses to live in the path of a hurricane? Dirtsiders should know better. You live on the marble, you get weather. The only weather we get out here is the occasional solar storm. And no matter how ferocious a solar storm gets, it can't knock the whirligig off its foundation. The gig doesn't even have a foundation. Just torque. But I sent James my commiserations anyway, I admitted I couldn't imagine how bad it must be for everyone and I wished there was something I could do.

When he wrote back, he said, "Please just keep in touch. You're my lucky star. I look up in the sky and I imagine I can see you up there looking down at me. I log onto the telescope views of the whirligig and I pretend you're looking out the window, looking at the Earth and imagining me looking up. Do me a favor. Go to the window at 6pm my time and wave. I'll be looking at the gig through a scope then and I'll pretend I can see you waving."

So I did, and he did, and it was sweet, so we kept on exchanging messages. Most of his messages were about how upset he was because of how upset his parents were and how every day was the same damn thing over and over again and he hated waiting in line for fresh water, he had to bring his own containers, and he hated how hot it was in the day and how cold it was at night. He said he envied me, living in space and not having to worry about earthquakes and sandstorms and hurricanes and all the other stuff a restless planet can throw at you, only the occasional solar flare, and with the right kind of shielding in place, even that couldn't hurt you too badly. At least it didn't throw you out of bed in the middle of the night and knock your house apart.

Somewhere in there, I thought I could help take his mind off how bad his situation was so I asked him to help me with a project. I said that I had to design…um, the perfect space habitat. It was part of my term project on cost-analysis. My job was to think of the most outrageous things you could put on a space station and then show how or why they were impractical, because these were things that dirtsiders—um, I mean people on the marble, sorry—would ask for, and I wanted to be able to explain why or why not in the simplest possible terms. And do you think you could help me with that? He wrote back yes.

So we started throwing ideas at each other—most of them silly and outrageous, even impractical. He knew a lot more about starside conditions than I thought. Even though he'd never been up the beanstalk, he knew all about the stuff they do for tourists at Geosynchronous Station. And he had an uncle who helped design the L4 Cylinder and even consulted on the L5, so he knew a lot about that too.

Then we talked about some of the bigger things the Chinese built for their permanent habitats on Luna and Mars. For their Dubai partners. Atriums, swimming pools, mile-high towers, jungle-gardens, forests, village walks, plazas, huge wilderness areas, even zoos and aquariums, lakes, rock-climbing walls, endless ski-slopes, full-size concert halls and theaters, Olympic quality gymnasiums, running tracks, shopping malls, enough stuff to fill a dozen whirligigs. James and I came up with two or three new designs every week, I drafted the outlines, he filled in the textures, we collaborated on the math. I didn't tell him that I was bringing each design to the dinner table for Ganny and Gampy to look at.

Ganny and Gampy knew he was helping me. As long as it was for a hypothetical space station for my fictional term project, it was all right. They wanted me to be ambitious, so they didn't mind a little collaboration. They were collaborating on some of their own ideas, so they couldn't very well object to James and I working together.

Every night, after we finished dinner, we sat around the table and presented our latest follies. That's what we called them. Follies. In the traditional sense of the word. We had one rule—the first response to every idea had to be an appreciation of how outrageous it was and how ambitious it was. After we applauded each idea for its sheer impracticality, we would add it to the list of things we would want on an ideal spaceship. Everything was added to the list. Everything. Nothing was ever dismissed as too silly. Not even Gampy's elephant or Ganny's Hundred Acre Wood. Or my own Wild Strawberry Fields.

Then, after we laid out the parameters of each astonishing addition, we'd give it to IRMA to run the math. How much lebensraum would it need? What kind of maintenance would be required? How much water? Oxygen? Power? Shielding? How much time would it take to construct? How much would it mass? How much payload penalty would we have to pay to include it? Balance all that against projected usage patterns. If we subtract it from the rest of the package, how much do we gain? Or lose? Everything was given a viability rating, a combined score, and we had a growing list of possibilities sorted by practicality all the way from must-have to violates-the-law-of-conservation-of-energy. Ultimately, our final decision would be where to put the dividing line, the cut-off point between yes and no. From day to day, the maybe zone fluctuated in size. Sometimes it was a big purple haze, sometimes a sharp maroon line. Mostly it was just a shallow band of magenta.

I knew what Gampy was doing, but I didn't mind. It was a great game. He was teaching me to regard every choice as a location on a vast map of possibilities. Consider all the overlapping sets, consider the locus of optimal points. Look for a balance between imagination and sensibility, between desire and practicality, and ultimately between capability and cost-effectiveness.

"I know what I want," Ganny announced one night. We both looked over to her. "I want a bathtub," she said with a voice of absolute finality. "A real old-fashioned bathtub. Round. Big enough to stretch out full length. Big enough for two. With water-massage jets. And sonics. And little champagne bubbles too. And...candles. And scented bubble-bath. And flowers." Her face went all dreamy for a moment.

"A bathtub?" That was me. It didn't sound practical. Why would you want a bathtub when a sonic-enhanced shower was far more efficient. It made no sense at all to me. Despite our rule against plonking, I asked, "Why?"

"Because," she said. And folded her arms.

Gampy smiled and told IRMA to add it to the design parameters. And rate it as critical-to-survival.

I turned seventeen and we began whittling our list. Practicality ruled. We didn't discard any ideas because they were dumb, only because they were impractical. For instance, we could have a ship's cat, if we wanted—we could afford the oxygen and water and food for a live animal—but it made more sense to fab a mechanical instead. Easier to train, a lot cleaner, and it would give us an extra set of mobile monitors that could get into small spaces; plus we'd get the same affectional bonus, and it would be a lot less expensive than having a tabby shipped out from Mars.

The same standards applied to all our choices. Yes, we could have a bigger lounge, a genuine salon with its own attendant plumbing, but it would have to serve double duty as a theater and a dining hall and a gymnasium with all the attendant gear folded away into the bulkheads, unfolding as needed. Yes, personals could be larger, but that would mean a smaller crew and more dependence on bots and intelligence engines. That was a null-brainer—a smaller biomass-to-biosupport ratio meant an expanded viability envelope, and an enhanced payload window. Better for everyone.

We had a keel. Actually, we had three keels in the junkyard, that mass of pods and leftover parts at the south end of the gig's axis. We even had what was left of Gampy's first boat. But it was obvious that Gampy wanted something bigger than that. Much bigger. He didn't say it aloud, but he was thinking about the old *Lysistrata*. He'd been talking about refitting her for years, ever since he'd claimed what was left of her for salvage. It made sense, the keel was still good and a lot of her internal harnesses still checked out, she just didn't have life support any more. And of course, she'd need new engines, but we had seven decades of new technology to draw upon. We could use a lot of the existing mountings, and where we needed to, we could strengthen her frame with a bigger set of harnesses. We'd end up with a stronger ship than the original designers had conceived.

Once we'd made that decision, the rest of the plan snapped into place like pieces of a jigsaw puzzle.

We had fifty years of stuff hanging in the junkyard and at least another twenty years of resupply for all the old buckets still crawling around the belt. Plus a few items we'd bought on consignment for resale to option-holders. We had an assortment of power plants, all kinds. We had flywheels, solar panels, fuel cells, hot-and-cold fusion reactors, and even a couple of old turbines. Equipment? All kinds. We had pipes and pumps and all sorts of electronics and monitors and bots and sensors. And engines? Lord, did we have engines, more than enough to grab an asteroid and drag it home. We had six different kinds of blast engines and more than enough tanks of high-velocity propellants to drive them. And if that wasn't enough we had solar sails, ion drives, plasma drives, mass-accelerators, and all the different kinds of spare parts necessary to repair those drives. We had all the stuff people used for throwing rocks around, all the stuff we leased to miners and comet-tossers and anyone else who wants to move a mountain. Best of all, we had the raw materials we needed to build at least a dozen traction units, and the keel of the *Lysistrata* was strong enough to hold them all. That's why Gampy wanted us to think extravagant. We were going to build one of the fastest, most powerful ships in the system.

We were halfway through the final design process, when Gampy died.

It wasn't anything heroic and it wasn't anything stupid. It was just what happened. He was working his way patiently around the centrifuge, using the cane because his knee hurt. He did that every shift after eating. Six times around and he'd stop at the red bench to catch his breath. This time, he couldn't. IRMA rang the alert and we all went screaming down the slidy-poles, scrambling and bouncing around the arc, but it was too late. The medi-bots already had him stretched out on the deck. Ganny pounded his chest and screamed at him. "Don't you dare leave me now, you son of a bitch! Not now!" She was really angry. But not at Gampy. At everything else, herself mostly. The medi-bots pushed her out of the way and did their medi-bot thing, but it wasn't enough. Gampy was already gone. His face was closed.

The funeral was simple. Gampy had friends all over the ecliptic and over a thousand of them logged in and shared their best memories. Rev Morgan holoed in from Mars to conduct the service and she was as eloquent as always. Of course, everybody had to allow for the time lag. Gampy didn't trust the so-called instantaneous transmissions of the quantum-channels, he used to say that the quantum-channels had to include all possible decryptions, so you couldn't really know if you were receiving the right one. I never knew if he was serious about that or not, I always thought it was because the quantum connections were too expensive to establish and too difficult to maintain, but Ganny said it was because Gampy regarded all instantaneous communication as a kind of electronic leash that anyone could yank whenever they felt like it. Maintaining distance in time and space was his way of staying independent of the demands of others—as much as possible. But anyway, there weren't any glitches in the time-delayed synchronizations and the service was beautiful. My favorite part was the requiem.

"For one brief moment, a piece of the universe comes alive, looks around, asks questions, explores, discovers, creates, connects—and in that moment, the almighty universe knows its own beauty. Whatever meaning life has, it is found in everything we create for ourselves and for others. From stardust we are born, to stardust we return. We commend this soul to the eternal sea in the sure and certain knowledge he will find his way safely home...." And then we freeze-dried him for the H2O, reduced the rest to little pieces, and plowed him into the soil beneath the rose bushes in Ganny's garden because that's what he'd always said he wanted us to do. Waste not, want not.

Of course, Ganny and I both sobbed our hearts out and held onto each other and bawled like babies. I remember being surprised at how small and thin she'd become. But she was still a core of strength and energy and I knew she wasn't going to be following Gampy any time soon. So I just collapsed into her embrace and let out all my grief and anguish in great racking screams of rage. And so did she. I was hoarse for two days after.

Three days in a row, we sat up late talking. All the stuff we usually kept to ourselves, only this time we just let it out, over and over. We talked about everything and nothing and how much we were going to miss Gampy and what we should do next, and Ganny admitted that she felt so much at a loss she didn't know what to do next. Should we continue building Gampy's spaceship or cut our losses now? Except that Gampy always knew what he was doing and he wouldn't want us to quit just because he wasn't here or we were afraid, but just the same, he wasn't here and we had to figure this out for ourselves. And then we hugged each other some more and cried some more and went on talking, just talking to talk, not because what we had to say was important, but because it was important that we said something. We talked like dirtsiders, but neither one of us cared, and for a while I even understood why dirtsiders talked so much. It was because they were so lonely inside their skins. Surrounded by all those people, they were still lonely. They had to do something desperate to try to connect. I knew we were being just as emotional but it was all right. We had the right to be emotional. Didn't we?

But there must be something about emotions that makes people *Stoopid* with a capital *stoo*. Gampy used to tell me that, all the time. Now I wished I'd listened better. Don't ever do anything while you're upset. Don't even make a decision. It's all right to be upset. Upset is a normal part of life. But upset is also stupid-time, so don't do anything or decide anything while you're in stupid time. That was the part I forgot.

Because while I was still so busy being upset about Ganny missing Gampy so badly, I made the mistake of checking my email, and there was a note from Jimmy Sawyer, how upset he was, because everything in Baja was falling apart and he wasn't going to be able to finish college because both his moms were out of work because there was no money to rebuild the hotels and the tourists were going down to Yucatan instead to watch the Howler monkey wars, which were a lot more interesting than watching *Cabaneros* fight over water and the best projections were that it would be seven to ten years before the local economy recovered, if it ever did, and they might have to apply for refugee assistance and move, but if they did that, they'd have to sign over what was left of his college fund and his moms would have to give up their pensions, but he just couldn't see any other way out of their predicament. They only had electricity for a few hours, only at night, and they were down to less than 2000 calories a day per person, they were hungry all the time, and that was on a good day, and none of them could afford to get any skinnier, especially him. He didn't have any energy anymore. Their situation just kept getting worse and worse, so bad that he was thinking about signing up for a mind-wipe/enlistment so his family would get the bonus. The only thing that kept him from doing that was that he didn't want to give up his relationship with me.

I wrote back, begging him to please not do anything stupid. I didn't want to lose him either. I told him what Gampy always said about not making decisions while you're scared or angry or afraid or so caught up in any emotion that you lose all sense of perspective. Please don't give up on yourself, I told him, because things have to get better eventually. They just have to. But I'm not sure I really believed that myself. The people on the marble just keep stumbling from one polycrisis to the next and they've so incorporated it into their way of life that stumbling through polycrises is their new normal.

Maybe that's why Gampy never wanted to keep close ties with dirtside. He didn't want to get pulled back down into the soup. So all I could do for Jimmy was keep on writing messages of encouragement. It left me feeling futile and helpless, but Ganny wouldn't let me send him any money. We had a rule about that and we'd never broken it, so all I could do for Jimmy was keep telling him how much I cared—and hope that would be enough. And even that made me feel bad, because now I felt responsible for his well-being. Jimmy had just told me that I was the only thing keeping him alive and that meant I was sorta stuck, wasn't I? I had to keep on being his friend, no matter what, because if I stopped caring then he would probably do something stupid. And then that would be my fault. Wouldn't it?

And that's when I made my bigger mistake. Somewhere in the middle of sending Jimmy back my sympathies and my concern and my caring, somewhere in there I told him I understood how he must feel, like there was no future anymore, and then I told him about Gampy dying and how much I missed him every day and how I felt so bad, maybe even the same way that Jimmy must feel about everything, because now my life was floating adrift, and all of our hard work making plans and everything might have been all for nothing, and maybe it was wrong for me to feel like that because it was selfish, because starsiders are supposed to take care of each other, what I really needed to do was take care of Ganny because she had to be feeling even worse than me. I told Jimmy I wished he was here so I could cry on his big beautiful shoulder and help me and Ganny figure out what to do next because all the help he'd given me on the spaceship design proved he was good at figuring things out, and even as I wrote that I knew I was starting to sound like a silly dirtsider girl, helpless and stupid and talking way too much. But the point was, and this is what I needed him to hear, no matter how bad Ganny felt, no matter how much she missed Gampy, she was still determined to keep going, no matter how bad things got. And if an old lady like Ganny had that kind of strength in her heart then I should be able to do that too. And if I could do it then a big strong guy like James should be able to find that kind of strength in his own heart as well. We weren't giving up on our plans and neither should he. Because what we say starside is that no matter how bad things might seem, as long as you're still breathing you're surviving. And as long as you're surviving, you're still in the game. And a bunch more stuff like that. Most of it stupid, but you get the idea. I didn't want him to get wiped and I'd say just about anything to keep him Jimmy.

And then immediately after I sent it I realized I'd said way way way too much about what was happening on the gig. I sent an instant-retrieve message right after it and hoped that the snatch-back would arrive in time, but you never know. It all depends on how quickly you send it and which way the packets are routed and whether or not the other person is sitting on the mailbox, opening things as fast as they arrive. Or if they have an agent doing that in case somebody sends a snatch-back. I dunno. There are a lot of different ways. The real trick is catching the message before it actually arrives.

Out among the flying mountains, it can take anywhere from ten minutes to two hours to get a message, depending how many big marbles and tin cans it has to bounce off. Traffic is a collection of ricochets. Anything with an antenna is part of the cloud. Sometimes the message-packets arrive from a dozen different directions, scattered and out of order. We once waited three days for an episode of Derby to finish downloading. Gampy might have liked his independence, but you pay a price for being a hermit-crab. So I didn't know for the better part of a shift if I'd caught the message to James in time. When the acknowledgment finally did come in, I felt like crying all over again, this time from relief. The snatch-back had arrived nine minutes after the target message, which had not yet been read. The target message was deleted, leaving only a stub acknowledging a message had been retrieved. That I could explain. I'd just have to figure out a suitable explanation. Excuse. Story. Lie. Whatever.

Except once I started thinking, the mind-mice started gnawing.

See, if James was really some kind of a data-pumping avatar, like Gampy once feared, then maybe the damage was already done. The message sat in his mailbox for nine minutes. That's more than enough time for a data-trap to capture a copy. And a data-trap lets the recipient examine

Hvednoct

a message without giving the sender any acknowledgment at all that it's actually been read. And if James really was a data-pumping avatar, then of course he'd have a data-trap, and of course he'd know what I'd said, even if he pretended he didn't. I'd have no way of knowing. Crap.

And that's the problem with being even a little bit suspicious. You start getting a lot suspicious. And then everything is suspect. And at the end, after you've finished distrusting everybody else—even your closest friends and family—you can't even trust yourself anymore. And I didn't know what kind of message to send to James to replace the one I didn't know if he'd seen or not.

But then things got real busy on the gig, because we had a shift change, and Ganny had to pay off some contracts she had been holding on consignment because without Gampy on the gig our credit rating went down a notch or six, which wasn't really fair because it was Ganny who managed the finances, but you can't argue with software because software doesn't listen. And it doesn't help to talk to a human being about it either because most dirtsiders are software-slaves, not willing to disagree with what the machinery says they can or can't do, which is why they're dirtsiders and doomed to stay that way forever. Slaves. "I'm sorry, we're not authorized to think for ourselves…."

And the Red Team, people we'd known for years, people who'd all professed their sincerest and deepest condolences only a few weeks before—they had the chutzpah to demand payment in advance. Ganny had to put a big chunk of liquidity into escrow before they'd board. And that didn't sit well with her. She understood the thinking, but things were strained for awhile. She'd always treated them like family, but now the union-rep was saying, "Yes, we appreciate that, don't take it personal, ma'am, it's just business." For the first couple of weeks, Ganny's menus were a little restrained. Her way of expressing her opinion about putting business above loyalty. Even though she knew they were right. We'd have done the same.

But without Gampy, we had to shift a lot of responsibilities around, so I ended up taking on most of the menu-planning and that helped a little bit. I didn't think it was fair to punish the red team with liver and onions every night, even though I understood why Ganny was miffed. Although I kinda like liver and onions, not everybody does. And there is such a thing as variety. And more important, food equals morale. Everybody knows that. So when I volunteered to take over the cooking, I wasn't just doing her a favor, I was doing everybody a favor. This was what Gampy would have wanted. Somebody taking care of things while Ganny put herself back together. Especially taking care of the crew.

Ganny would settle down eventually, she always did, but this time she might need a few extra weeks. When she found out the blue crew wasn't coming back—they'd signed a new contract elsewhere—she disappeared for three shifts, not even answering my calls to dinner. When she finally did come out, her face had a new hardness to it. I didn't ask.

I figured she was still hurting a lot inside and because she didn't have anybody to blame, she couldn't help herself, she just took it out on convenient targets. Even me, a few times. I mean, I'd lost my Gampy, but she'd lost the whole other half of her life. So she was powerfully upset— upset isn't even a good enough word to describe what she was going through, but she was upset enough to forget Gampy's instructions about not making decisions while you're upset. She always apologized afterward, but we were both getting used to the idea that things were going to be a lot different now. We were going to have to build a lot more bots to replace the live crewmembers, but in the long run that would probably be better for our bottom line. We could have switched a long time ago, but Gampy had a rule against giving people's jobs to machines, because machines didn't have families to support, but now that the crews were quitting, without even giving us much notice, we weren't really obligated any more, were we? But then, while we were still sorting that one out, preparing to fab three dozen new bots, the rest of the bad news arrived.

Behind Ganny's back, the dirtside sons of bitches at Payload, Inc. negotiated new contracts with half the belters in the arc. Instead of transshipping through the whirligig, they were going to whirl the pods direct to the customers. Most customers didn't have whirligigs or even the resources to create a spindizzy, a spinning tether. So the pods would have to carry fuel for deceleration and that meant a corresponding reduction in payload, but if they threw the pods from a lower point on the beanstalk, that would reduce their outbound speed and also the amount of fuel they'd have to carry for deceleration. But the slower speed also meant the pods would be in transit a lot longer, some as long as three or four or even five years. But the price difference was still enough to be competitive. And it would have been mostly legal, except for the part that wasn't.

See, almost all of that cargo had already been bought on margin by Gampy. It was his. Ours. Ganny's. But the dirt-lovers had simply cancelled their side of the deal. Oh, they'd done it nice and legal. They'd put Payload, Inc. into receivership, then sold it to themselves at a three cents on the dollar, just enough to pay off the lawyers, and resold the cargo contracts to themselves for even less. Ganny filed claims—on Earth, Luna, and Mars. The Earth court dismissed it, the Luna tribunal refused to hear the case, the Martian judge ruled that Ganny had a claim, but he had no authority to enforce it against an Earthside company.

Meanwhile the new company, Free Ride, Inc., negotiated half-price deals with all of our customers, so low that even our best friends couldn't resist. So nearly a trillion dollars of Ganny's property was now scheduled to go everywhere but here. Free Ride could afford to be generous with their pricing because they were selling our stolen property to our stolen customers. Later on, once they'd driven us out of business they'd own the market and they could raise prices to whatever they wanted.

Ganny knows how to cuss in sixteen languages, including a couple of dead ones, she might be the last person alive who knows how to swear in Pascal, whatever that is, that's something else I have to look up. Ganny can go on for a long time before repeating herself. I didn't need to know what all those different words meant to understand what she was saying. A certain Mister I-Won't-Say-His-Name-Aloud should have been grateful that he had 330 mega-klicks of vacuum between himself and Ganny, otherwise he would have lost a couple pieces of his anatomy and was probably very fond of. Okay, that's theoretical on my part, I have the genotype, but not the phenotype, which means I never had any, and even if I had I still would have traded them for the parts I have instead which I like a lot better, I mean, I never understood why anyone would even want all that stuff attached and hanging around and getting in the way. What a nuisance. Ganny says she used to feel that way too, but that was before she met Gampy, and someday I'll probably feel different too. So she says. That's nice, Ganny, but way out here in the belt, that's about as likely as giant space amoebas eating Jupiter. Again.

Ganny didn't stop cussing. Not this time. Not even when the IRMA unit told her that she was raising the temperature in the main cabin to critical levels and that the refrigeration units were threatening to fail. Sometime before he died, Gampy had programmed the IRMA unit's social interface with a supercharged sarcasm function, that being the only way to catch Ganny's attention when she went off on one of her rants. Usually that kind of interruption was enough. This time no.

Ganny's rants were impressive. When I was little, they terrified me even though I was never the target. But then Gampy explained to me about performance art, and once I recognized that Ganny's tantrums were for her own enjoyment, I would go and make popcorn and Gampy and I would sit back and enjoy the show. When Ganny would finally inevitably run down, Gampy would say something like, "Not bad. I give it a six. You lost points when you recycled your previous extrapolations of mangled DNA in the ancestry of the reptilian cortex. But I did enjoy the stylistic expansions of neo-Germanic linguistic conjugations." And Ganny would reply something like, "Hmp, that was easily a seven point nine. You should have seen it from my side." Then she'd take a deep breath and that usually indicated that she was finished, and then she'd ask him what he wanted for dinner. And while he was saying, "How about something special tonight?" she was already asking, "Okay, so what do we do next?" And then, in unison, they'd both say, "I'm thinking it over...." And sometimes they'd even laugh. But after a while, they'd both figure something out together.

But Gampy was gone and Ganny wasn't going to stop ranting no matter how sarcastic the IRMA unit became because this nasty news was pretty much a declaration of war, arriving exactly one year to the day after Gampy's death. The bastards knew exactly what they were doing.

Ganny spent half a shift talking to Gampy's picture. "You son of a bitch. You picked the worst damn time to die. I need you so much. Now more than ever. This is one hell of a mess. You should have told me what to expect, what to do! You knew this was coming. And we promised not to drop any more capsules into the Pacific Ocean, so what am I supposed to do now?" She sent out a few messages to Gampy's most trusted friends, but she didn't find the replies all that encouraging. The dirtsiders were cutting off the money. And they hadn't moved capriciously. They'd spent years setting this up. Ever since the Pacific accident. This was their revenge.

What they didn't know was Ganny. Maybe they figured they were dealing with a silly old space-lady who kept her collection of pancakes in the airlock. Maybe they figured that without a man to tell her what to do, she'd just fall apart. Dirtside males can be so stupid and arrogant sometimes. What they didn't know was that Ganny had her own set of testicles. She showed them to me once, she kept them in the cryo-freezer. (Some other time I'll explain why it's a good idea to have both an X and a Y chromosome, even if you put the Y on the shelf and never use it. But I'm still not convinced I want a pair of my own.)

Oh yeah, I did a little ranting myself too. I didn't see much point in it, it didn't make me feel any better, but after Ganny and I stomped around the centrifuge a few times, we both felt silly enough to fall down laughing, so that had to count for something. But finally, after we both stopped laughing, we just looked at each other and said, in unison, "Okay, so what do we do next?" And then in unison, we both replied, "I'm thinking it over…." And then we started laughing again, this time so hard I almost wet my panties.

"All right," said Ganny, "Consider this. We finish the spaceship anyway. We can finish installing engines on the keel, attach a few life-support and fuel pods, hunker down in a pod like the old-fashioned astronauts, go to Mars, and pick up the life-support module. And then…we'll go pick up our property, every pod in transit. We'll do a local spindizzy and sling it long way around to the gig. Then we head back to the gig and catch the balls we've thrown."

"Is that legal?"

Ganny shrugged. "As legal as it needs to be. We have the Martian judgment in our pocket. That's our authorization. What are they going to do to us?"

Somewhere in there, the conversation passed *if*, and went straight to *when*. "Can we build the ship in time?"

"All depends on how many bots we can fab. I figure we can put a hundred to work within two months. We can have bots building bots until we pass the point of diminishing returns."

So Ganny and I sat down in front of the big display and studied orbits, trajectories, hyperbolas, parabolas, ellipses, and even what occasionally passed for a straight line. Of course, no straight line ever went unpunished. The shortest distance between two puns is a straight line. The good news was that the damned blue marble was heading around the backside of Sol, so anything they launched could take as long as five or six years to get to our side of the belt. We had a pretty big window to pick off the pods and send them home.

Then the other shoe dropped. I don't know why dirtsiders are always dropping shoes, but they do. And this time it was a pretty big one. The Martian Electric Boat Company cancelled our order for a life-support module.

They said it wasn't us, it was them. Yeah, right. They said that changing market conditions required them to reevaluate their customer base. They said that the growing needs of their corporate customers required them to focus on standardized modules. They said their heuristic analysis of our readjusted profit position projected that we would not be able to complete the contract satisfactorily. They said everything except "we are not authorized to think for ourselves."

Right.

I knew it was serious when Ganny didn't say a single bad word. She just sank down into a chair and put her head in her hands. She didn't say anything for a long long time. And I knew better than to say anything to her. I got up and made tea. The good kind. I poured two cups and pushed one in front of her. She ignored it.

"Ganny?"

She looked up. She looked broken.

"They figured it out. They can't allow us to build a spaceship." She let out a long sigh. She looked at the mug of tea in front of her as if she was seeing it for the very first time. But she didn't pick it up. "I don't know what to do. We're done. All our plans—" She put her head back into her hands.

Somebody, somewhere had figured it out. Ganny did too have the stones to finish what Gampy started. So they weren't going to take any chances. They'd bought up the entire run of hulls from the Martians for the next seven years. They hadn't just stopped us. They'd stopped *all* the potential competition.

Oh. Crap. And double-crap.

He *had* used me.

I sent James an email. "You bottom-feeding dirtsider! You filthy lying phony! If I could get my hands on you, I'd slap your ugly freckly face so hard it wouldn't stop spinning until it was on the back of your head. For all I care, you can mind-wipe your skinny ass into a rainbow brothel, getting happily cyber-fucked by anyone with two plastic dollars for the coin-slot on a public library terminal! I never want to hear from you again! Go frag yourself!" And this time I didn't snatch it back. I put a block on my inbox so he couldn't reply. But I was nowhere near as mad at him as I was at me. This was all my fault. Me and my big stoo-pid mouth. Frack.

After I finished beating myself up, I went and cried in Ganny's arms. I told her everything. I thought she'd be angry, but she wasn't. She just patted my hair, stroked my cheek, and told me not to worry about it, the blood was already in the water, the sharks had been circling for years, it would have happened anyway. And we were going to have to make the same difficult decision sooner or later, might as well be sooner. Then she told me the rest. She was getting buyout offers and she had to make up her mind which one to accept.

I pulled away and looked at her. Shocked. "But where will we go? The whirligig is all we have."

"I was thinking Mars...."

"Mars! No fracking way. Those people are dirtsider-wannabes. You can't trust them. We can't go there. Not after they've stolen our spaceship. They'll all be laughing at us. Or worse. They'll feel sorry for us for not being big strong men. What would Gampy say?"

"He's not here, sweetheart. We have to make up our own minds what's best."

"Well, Mars isn't! No way. Why don't we just stay on the whirligig? We're self-sufficient, we don't need anything from anyone else. And if we do, we just have them put it in the pipeline."

"Sweetheart, that's the point. We can't depend on the pipeline anymore."

"No! They can't do that. Too many people depend on us."

"Only for the cargo still in transit. After that's gone, we're pretty much done. You've seen the schedules. Gampy knew this was going to happen someday, even without the theft of our cargo. That's why he wanted to build a ship. You've seen the projections. The penetration of traction drives in the ecliptic will be 40% within six years. As fast as they can push the pieces up the beanstalks. It'll be 60% for cargo ships. 80% for bot-driven pods. Without a meat-crew, a big-enough tractor could accelerate continuously at 25 gee. If they can get direct delivery faster and cheaper from a tractor, people aren't going to use the pipeline. The whirligig will be just another piece of nostalgia. Like the pony express. That's what this is all about. The people who stopped us, don't want anyone competing with the shipping monopoly they're building. Don't take it personal. It's like the Red Crew. It's just business."

"But, Ganny—!"

"Sweetheart—we can go to Mars. You can go to college."

"I can go to college from here."

"You can meet a nice boy."

"Like Jimmy Sawyer? No thanks. I'm done with boys."

"You say that now—"

"My vibrator doesn't lie to me!"

Ganny didn't want to answer that one directly. Instead she softened her tone and expanded the context. "Starling, there's a whole universe of possibilities out there—"

It didn't work. "I like it *here!*" Okay, so I sounded like a spoiled dirtsider brat, but it was honest. Right then and there I didn't want any other possibilities. I wanted what I already had.

"Honey, this is the best we can do—"

"No, it isn't. This is giving up."

"Sweetheart, there isn't going to be anything left. We need to get out now, while we can still get out with a little bit of money. And pride."

"And then what? Sit around and knit?"

"Me? Knit? Gampy would come back from the grave just to see that. No, I don't think so. I'm just trying to make the best of a bad situation for us."

"No, you're not. You're giving up. And I won't have it." I pushed myself off and sailed out of the room. It's hard to slam a door in free fall, don't even try. You can't even swim away with an attitude. It just doesn't work. The best you can do is swim away, scowling.

Of course, I knew I was wrong. I was being angry—and stupid. You can't fight the laws of physics. You can't even negotiate with them. Gampy used to say, "The coyote *always* goes splat. Remember that." But I still didn't see why we had to give up our home. Gampy wouldn't give up. And he wouldn't let us give up either. The coyote usually goes a long long way before he finally splats. That had to count for something. There had to be a way. I just couldn't see it yet. And Ganny was probably having the same conversation in her head too.

If neither of us could see it, maybe it wasn't there.

Except I already knew what Gampy would say to that. "If it isn't there, you haven't created it yet."

I went down to the centrifuge. And paced. One good thing about the centrifuge, it's a good place to stomp around in anger. In fact, it's the only place you can stomp around in anger. When I was little, Gampy and I would make topsoil. The bots would dump a mix of manure and compost and mulch and fungus and pureed garbage and mineral dust and asteroid shavings into the pit. We'd add water and then we'd jump in and stomp up a storm. Whenever I was in a big sulk that lasted more than a day, Gampy would suddenly announce a need to make more topsoil. We'd stomp ourselves silly until we were both laughing so hard I'd forgotten why I was angry. Then we'd seed the whole mess with earthworms, shower off and consider it a job well done. I wished he was here now. We'd stomp up enough soil for a wheatfield.

We made soil mostly in the smaller pools. We'd mix in all kinds of grass and wildflower seeds and how high they grew would tell us how good the soil was. Gampy wouldn't plant crops until the soil was good enough. Once he got so frustrated with a particularly stubborn mix, he had everybody defecate into that tank for a week. Two weeks. Until something green finally poked a leaf up.

When we weren't making soil, we raised koi, big beautiful orange and white fish. They shimmered like liquid metal. Water is the most convenient ballast you can have in space. You pump it wherever you need weight. We used it to balance the centrifuge, with tanks of various sizes anchored all around the circumference, but we had three big pools, spaced 120 degrees apart. They were the primary reservoirs and they were almost always full. The only time I saw the levels go down even a little bit was when Gampy pumped a couple thousand gallons into a pod and slung it out to one of the ships prepping for the long ride. Gampy said that the most important thing you ever want to pack was water, lots of it.

The big pools were only a two meters deep, and for the first half of my life I was terrified of them. Probably because for the first half of my life I was shorter than two meters. Even today, I don't believe in free range water. Water belongs in tanks and bulbs, not sloshing around in the open like amoebas without skin. Gampy told me that swimming was fun, but the first time he tried to take me in the pool I shrieked like a rabid banshee. (Ganny showed me the video-logs.)

Gampy said that I needed to learn how to swim, but I didn't see the use of it. I wasn't going anywhere I'd ever need that particular skill. But Gampy didn't force the issue. Instead he made me a canoe. He found a bundle of plastic rods and tied two of them together at the ends. Then he put four cross-braces between them, arcing them out to form a canoe shape. Then he wrapped the frame with a wide sheet of transparent plastic wrap and a little bit of ribbon tape to hold the wrap in place. The boat was so light I could pick it up in one hand. He had to put a couple of keel-weights hanging from the bottom so it wouldn't tip too easily. Then he tied a rope to one end of it and the other end to the railing around the pool. Then he put the canoe in the water and showed me how it would float.

For the first hour, I wouldn't even climb into it. Not even with a life jacket and an inner tube around my waist. I just kept pushing it away and pulling it back. I did like how I could see through the bottom and see the koi a lot clearer and that's probably why I eventually climbed in. Not to paddle around, only to get a better view of the fish. I kept a tight hold on the rope and kept myself tightly pulled up against the side of the pool. But after a while, I did let myself drift out a little and then I pulled myself back quickly, and then after a while more, I'd push off and pull myself back again. And then when I thought no one was looking, I grabbed the paddle that Gampy had made—a rod with a plastic-wrapped loop at the end— and paddled myself around.

Of course, Gampy was watching the whole time. Mostly on the monitors in the lounge, just spinward up the arc of the 'fuge, but occasionally he'd stroll by and ask me how I was doing. At first I didn't say anything, not wanting to concede that he was right, but eventually I gave him a grudging "fine." A couple days later, he'd fabbed some fins and a snorkel and a mask and a paddle board, showed me how they all worked and let me teach myself how to swim. Not because he told me it was something I had to do, but because it was a better way to look at the koi close up.

Now, all these years later, walking around the centrifuge, stomping along the deck, the smell of the koi ponds still made me think of Gampy. I still had the canoe. I hadn't used it in years, I had long outgrown it, but I'd hung it up next to the pool with my fins and mask and snorkel as trophies. Or reminders. That's where I was sitting when Ganny finally came after me. She looked so sad I started crying. We grabbed each other in a tight hug and fumbled our apologies out, both at the same time.

"Ganny, I'm so sorry!"

"So am I, sweetheart. I've been so wrapped up in my own pain I wasn't thinking. I should have talked to you before this."

"No. I mean, yes. Okay. I'm sorry for being so emotional. I'm supposed to know better."

We sat down on the bench next to the pool and held hands for a while, neither of us speaking. Ganny looked up at the old canoe, hanging on the rack we used for towels and tools and whatever, and made a chuckling sound deep in her throat. "It's still watertight," I said. "After all these years. I still put it in the water sometimes. And it still floats. Gampy knew what he was doing."

"Yes, he did." She patted my hand. "He knew better than to force you."

We sat there a while longer and finally I said, "Remember when we first talked about the spaceship? The first time? With Gampy and everyone at the table? We talked about building the LSM ourselves. We ran the math on it, it wasn't impossible. It just wasn't as cost-effective. But…well, maybe we should think about it again."

Ganny didn't answer. She was still staring at the canoe. Still thinking about Gampy and all his little tricks. I wanted to distract her, get her back on purpose, thinking of solutions.

"I mean, we can fab all the parts we need, can't we? So who cares if it takes a little longer? We can still do it. We can show those damn Martians. Can't we, Ganny?"

She took a deep breath, one of those deep deep sighs that can mean anything from "I give up" to "I see your point" to "I've made up my mind." Or maybe nothing at all except "I need to catch my breath and think." But she squeezed my hand and I could tell she was thinking it over.

She started to shake her head, then stopped herself. I watched as her face went through a whole series of contradictory expressions. Yes. No. Maybe. Try this on for size. No, that won't work. Maybe. But it's a stupid idea. But Gampy would have liked it. No, I'm being silly. Well, silly is what got us out here in the first place. Remember? No, it's just too big. That never stopped us before. What am I thinking? I'm over a hundred years old. So what? Wouldn't you like to spit in their eye one more time? And wouldn't it be better to go down fighting than give up without a whimper? But I have to think about Starling's future too. This is her inheritance. But what else is she going to inherit from me? Resignation or determination? I don't know. Do I dare? Would it be fair to her? Would it be fair not to? But how would we do it anyway? I shouldn't make any decision until I run the numbers. Again? How many times do I have to run them? I've already run them a hundred times over, I don't have to run the numbers again. It's just so damned— No, it isn't. It's the mechanics of the job that's so frustrating, not the commitment—

Or maybe I was misreading the whole series of her expressions. Ganny brushed her hair back off her forehead, a useless gesture, her hair went right back where it wanted to go. She stood up and faced the rack with the canoe, reached out and picked it off the hook. She turned it over and over in her hands. It looked like she was trying to distract herself from tomorrow by focusing on yesterday. I wanted to scream in frustration. It looked like she was giving up.

Abruptly, Ganny turned to face me. "Go start dinner. I'm going for a walk." Translation: "I have to think about this."

It was a good sign. Or maybe it wasn't. Maybe what she had to think about was how to let me down easy. Maybe she needed to say goodbye to her gardens. Or maybe she really did need to think it over. I couldn't tell what she was thinking and I was usually pretty good at it.

But Ganny hadn't come down into the centrifuge since Gampy died, so it meant something. This was where Ganny and Gampy did their best work, walking and talking and holding hands like puppy-struck tweens. They were so cute when they did that.

I understood why she wanted to be alone now. She wanted to talk things out with Gampy one more time. This time she'd have to do both sides of the conversation, but she knew Gampy so well, she probably could. Ohell, I already knew what Gampy would say and so did Ganny. But she still needed to walk it out and talk it out, because that was the way they always did things. Together. That part, I envied. If I ever met a boy who was good at that, I might reconsider my decision. But it wouldn't be scummy Jimmy Sawyer, the big fat fake, whoever he was. Probably some morbidly obese dirty oldphart, sitting naked at his keyboard, a six-pack on the desk, cackling to himself how he data-pumped a naïve little starflake. What was that line from Shakespeare anyway? Revenge is a dish best served old? I didn't have to get even now, but I would get even. Count on it. Hell hath no fury like a woman, scorned or not. I'd have pictures of his little tiny penis posted from here to Andromeda if that's what it took.

The centrifuge has four decks, the top one is Lunar gravity and we use it mostly for crops. The next-to-bottom one is Earth gravity, and the maintenance level beneath that is 1.2 gee, useful for exercise, but very tiring. The second level is Martian gravity and it has our living and guest quarters, where we sleep and eat and work and exercise—and sometimes just hang out. The galley is on the second level too. You can make some really marvelous soufflés in 0.38 gee. And angel food cake so light it practically floats. But tonight, I made noodles and green sauce. I like the *al dente*, and I like the way all the different flavors of the different spices mix together, all sweet and tangy and rich to the point of shameful opulence. It's not one of Ganny's favorite recipes, but it's my personal comfort food. One of my personals. For some reason, it always makes me think of…people I was too young to miss when they went missing. Maybe someday I'd figure out why.

Ganny came into the kitchen while I was mixing the sauce, I had a metal whisk that scraped round and round against the stainless bowl with a satisfying rasp. When Ganny came in, I stopped. She had a frown on her face. She looked annoyed. "I almost had it. I almost did. Damn."

"Had what?"

She shook her head. "Nothing, it doesn't matter anymore. I don't have any…knitting needles."

"Huh?"

"I don't have any spokes."

"Spokes for what?"

But Ganny didn't answer. She was staring at…the whisk in my hand. She reached over and took it from me as if she'd never seen it before. She held it up before her eyes, still frowning, and spun it slowly between her fingers. A drop of green sauce separated itself and drifted lazily to the deck.

"Ganny?"

"I am *so* stupid," she announced. "I don't need knitting needles at all." She handed me back the whisk and bounced out.

"Um, dinner will be ready in fifteen—" I called after her.

"That's all the time I need—" She headed up the corridor to her office. I didn't know what she'd figured out, but it had to be something important. Ganny never put work before meals. "Work will always wait for you," she said. "If a problem is that big, it isn't going to go away. Eat first. Take care of your well-being so you can wrassle the problem down with all your strength." And so on. So, seeing her ignore her own advice was worth a couple of raised eyebrows. But the sauce needed stirring, and I knew she'd tell me what she was thinking as soon as she was through thinking it, so I just went back to work.

Over dinner, it was just Ganny and me tonight, Ganny wouldn't eat with the red team anymore, she broke a family rule, she began talking business. I started to correct her, but she shook her head. "Gampy isn't here, sweetheart. We get to make new rules if we want. And besides, this is important. Mm, your green sauce is just right tonight. You did good." She waved at the display with her fork, bringing it to life. "See, here's the

51

problem, and I think Gampy knew it all along—what we have, we have a lot of. What we don't have, we don't have any. So whatever we do, we have to do it with what's on hand. Because I suspect whatever we try to order, it probably isn't going to get here. Here—"

As she talked, the display assembled all of the various pieces of the proposed ship. The keel of the *Lysistrata* looked like a spear, but now with a shielded bulb instead of a point—the forward observatory and radar disc. The plasma drives and the accelerators were a thick bundle of thinner rods wrapped around the body of the spear. At the aft end of the schematic, the tractors clicked into place, looking like oversized feathers on a shuttlecock. "Now, we've got the raw material. We can spin out a radiation shield—" A large disc whirled into existence just ahead of the feathers. "The only thing we don't have is a doughnut. A life-support system." On the display, colored in red, a doughnut shaped module slid down the spear and parked itself just in front of the disc of the radiation shield. "Without a doughnut, we're not going anywhere."

"We had this conversation already. With Gampy. Remember?"

"Yes, sweetheart. But I wanted to restate the problem so you could see if I left anything out."

I shook my head. "This is where I always get stuck too. We don't have enough raw material to fab a hull or deck plates or bulkheads."

"Yes, we do. We just don't know it."

"All we have is beanstalk cable. A lot of it."

"Yes, that's what I said."

"You just lost me."

"Sorry, sweetheart. Usually, you're half a jump ahead of me. There's an idea that's been rattling around inside my head for a while. Nobody's ever done it, because nobody's ever had to, but IRMA says it could work, the numbers all crunch."

I made the mistake of interrupting. "I was thinking maybe we could put the whirligig on the spear—?"

"No, I already thought of that. The gig has too much mass. The torque would make it almost impossible to turn. Even if we throw away the ballast rocks."

"Put a gimbal in the keel? Put the engines on a swiveling axis—"

"Still too much mass to push. And too much strain on the swivel joint. No, there's something easier. Look—" She pointed at the display again. "We're going to knit a spaceship. Without knitting needles."

"Huh—?" For a moment I thought she'd popped a seal. The strain of everything had finally gotten to her. I was genuinely scared for both of us. But no—

Ganny pointed her fork at the display. "IRMA, show Starling how to knit a doughnut."

I watched as the display ran Ganny's schematic. It wasn't fancy, it was mostly blueprint, but it was impressive as hell. As soon as I figured out what she was thinking, I started getting enthusiastic. It was crazy, but it wasn't *that* crazy. If we did it right, it would work.

"Wow," I finally said when I was coherent again. "I'd sure like to see the look on their faces when we arrive at Martian orbit with *that*."

"Or even Earth," said Ganny. "You want to visit the big blue marble?"

It wasn't exactly a chill, more like a rush of fear and anticipation, but it did go up my spine and then right back down again. So maybe it was a chill. The marble? Hell, yes! And not just because there was a big freckled nose I wanted to punch.

"Ganny, that'll be the biggest ship in the ecliptic. Even bigger than the one Gampy designed. Bigger even than some of the ships going out on the long ride. You could plant a whole farm—"

"Uh-huh. That's the idea. We'll have to start cracking gas immediately. That's another problem. How are we going to get enough air pressure to boil water for soup? But I have an idea on that one too. But I need you to study this. See if I've missed anything."

Ganny hadn't missed much. There was only one big change that I suggested. "We need two doughnuts so we can rotate them in opposite directions—so they cancel each other's torque. That makes us much more maneuverable. More important, that gives us two independent life-support modules. Remember what happened to the *Ballista?*"

"That will double our cost—"

"In materials, yes. But it's not that much when you think about it. And we'll have the bots for it, more than enough, they're already growing in the fabbers. And they'll work 24/7 with Saturdays off for prayers and maintenance."

"Probably more prayers than maintenance." Ganny smiled. "But go on."

"There's another advantage. We can stagger the construction, kind of like an assembly line. Once you configure a bot for a job on one wheel, you already have it configured for the same job on the other. As soon as it finishes its task on one doughnut, it goes to the other. Also, I think we should triple hull. At least. Maybe more. Maybe six times over the engineering requirements."

Ganny was following and nodding until I got to that last part. "Isn't that a little extreme?"

"Uh-uh. See, the thing is—if I were a dirtsider, I'd be terrified of this hull. Even not being a dirtsider, it gives me the cold shimmies. We have to have unquestionable hull-integrity. Everybody who hears about how this ship is built is going to think we're crazy. At least until they think about it. It's like the first time someone said, 'why not drop a cable from space and run elevators up and down?' It defies common sense, or what passes for common sense on the marble. So we have to out-think their disbelief— what Gampy called their visceral-skepticism. And not just theirs. Ours as well. Like when they finally did drop a beanstalk, they had to make it six times stronger than their own math said was necessary. Just to be sure— in case they were wrong."

Ganny held my argument up to the light and looked at it carefully. She turned it over and over and over, much more than she needed to. But she understood what I was really saying. When you're working with human beings, you're not talking about rationality. You're talking about belief systems. Everybody has one. Especially the people who believe they're objective. So you don't just build for functionality, you build for the kind of certainty that goes way beyond what people already believe. Triple hull. At least. Triple-triple hull.

Finally, Ganny nodded. "It makes sense for a lot of reasons, especially the ones we won't know about until afterwards. Let's run it through IRMA and see what she says."

"Ganny?"

"Yes, punkin?"

"Once we start, we're not going to be able to keep it secret. There are telescopes trained on us."

"Yes, I know."

"Is there any way we can flummox them?"

"Probably not." Then she smiled. "But think about this. Once we start the whole thing spinning, that'll be flummox enough. By the time anyone figures it out, we'll be less than six months from completion."

"But what if they try to stop us? They've already hired away both our crews and cancelled our Martian order. What if they...I don't know...threw a rock at us or something?"

"Mm." Ganny put her fork down. She cupped her hands as if she was about to say a prayer and rested her chin in them. Her eyes went far away for a moment or six. "Okay," she finally said. "Try this. We'll attach the keel to the axis of the whirligig, so it looks like we're extending the gig. We'll mate the *Lysistrata*'s forward airlock to the bottom-cluster. To the big cargo lock. Now, when people ask what we're doing, we announce that we're changing our plans. We're not going to build a spaceship after all, it's not cost-effective, that market niche doesn't work for us, but we recognize

55

the growth potential—blah blah blah—for the next fifteen years as more and more ships are equipped with traction drives, so we're going to expand the gig to accommodate that growing market. Tractor ships are going to put the whole solar system within easy reach, so we're building a grand new gambling resort for all the rich tourists looking for an out-of-any-world vacation experience. Plus, we'll also continue to provide supply and slingshot services for colonists. Does that make sense to you, so far?" I nodded. Ganny went on. "So...we build three doughnuts. Two are counter-rotating LSMs, we'll be honest about that, but the third will be a dummy, to hide the engines we're assembling. We'll say it's our new machine shop, our construction base, which won't really be a lie, we just won't say what kind of machines we're fabbing. Nobody will know we're assembling a spaceship until we undock, unfold, and light up the engines. What do you think?"

"I like it," I said. "I think Gampy would too."

"I know he would." Ganny looked pleased, even satisfied. She liked having a plan. She liked having a big plan. "We'll have to run the numbers through IRMA. This is going to require some tricky project planning, but it'll work. It will work." She reached over and patted my hand. "We did good. You did good. We deserve a treat. Chocolate ice cream! With hot fudge!"

We topped it off with a dollop of gleeful dishing at the expense of MEBC. And then some exuberant fantasizing. After all, if we could do it once, we could do it a many times. We could even go into competition with MEBC. Our materials cost would be significantly less, our production lines could be faster, our per-unit cost would be cheaper, our modules would have no size limitations—

"We'll have to file a patent application—"

"But we won't mention shipcraft applications in the first patents, just expansion modules. We'll file a separate set just before we launch—"

Abruptly, we both looked at each other and stopped laughing. If the first one worked, we *could* build more. We could do it. And revenge is a dish best served *bold*. We left the dishes for a bot to clear and headed straight up to the office, giggling like a slumber party looking for a place to happen.

See, the problem was that once somebody does something, everybody else thinks that's the only way to do the same thing. Spaceship design is still stuck in the twenty-first century. Sure, the individual bits and pieces of technology have improved, the materials are better, but everybody still uses the same old-fashioned design. Build a long strong keel. Attach engines at one end, life-support doughnuts at the other. Add supply pods, equipment pods, ballast pods wherever they fit. Your ship looks like a cluster of grapes on a stick, with solar wings and heat radiators sticking out wherever.

Most ships start at the bottom of a gravity well. Earth or Mars. Wherever you can put down a factory without the neighbors complaining about the noise. All the different parts are manufactured in pieces, sent up the beanstalk, and assembled in space. So they're made—designed that way—to withstand gravity as well as thrust. If you build the pieces in space, you only have to design them for thrust. And if you're never thrusting more than a fraction of a gee, your engineering can be a lot different than if your pods are coming up the elevator at a thousand klicks an hour.

In space, you design for tensile strength and connectivity and hull integrity. You don't have to waste a lot of mass on heat shields and heavy plating and cross-bracing and all the other things that gravity and atmosphere demand. That's what Ganny figured out. Looking at the little canoe that Gampy put together for me in an afternoon, Ganny started wondering, "Why can't we build a life-support module the same way?" Build a frame and wrap it in plastic sheeting. Or even ribbon tape. Instant hull. Cheap. Easy.

What stopped her wasn't the plastic, but the frame. We didn't have one. We didn't have the materials to build one. We'd need to build a great big wheel. Very sturdy. One that would rotate and withstand the strain of centrifugal "gravity." You lay down floor plates and then you put the bots to work, fabbing reels of plastic and wrapping it round and round and round until you had enough layers to feel secure. But we didn't have a frame and we didn't have the manufacturing capability to fab one. And even if we did, we still didn't have hull plates or the way to build those either. Constructing the fabbers to build either of those things could take as long as three years, maybe as much as five. And we'd still need raw materials. Cannibalizing the junkyard—we'd have to build a shredder and a refinery and all kinds of separators and at least three dozen bots to run the equipment. Not cost-effective. Gampy was right. And probably somebody at MEBC had done all the same math and figured out how to put us out of business with a single phone call.

Then Ganny saw the whisk in my hand and she saw something nobody else saw. As Gampy would say, they didn't see it because they didn't believe it. But Ganny was already halfway there. We didn't need to build a rigid frame. We could *spin* one. It was so simple it was embarrassing. What did we have a lot of? Cable, ribbon tape, plastic wrap. And more cable. Lots of cable. Enough cable to rebuild the whirligig several times over. Enough cable to rebuild a couple dozen whirligigs, which was Gampy's original idea. Don't go out mining for gold, just sell shovels to those who do. You'll make a lot more money.

Think of a sling. Whirl it fast enough and centrifugal force will keep the sling rigid for as long as you spin it. Just don't stop spinning.

Start with a hub. It looks like the rim inside an automobile tire. Put the hub on the axis of the keel. The keel of the *Lysistrata* already had a half dozen hubs in place from its previous incarnation, so we were already set for the next step. Attach one end of a long cable to the top rim on the hub, attach the other end of the same cable to the matching spot on the bottom rim. Attach some weights to the cable, space them as far apart as you want your wheel to be thick. Do this at least three or four dozen times until you have looping cables all the way around. Kind of like the kitchen whisk, only loose.

Now you spin the hub. Get it rotating nice and fast. As the whole thing whirls, the keel-weights fly outward to their farthest possible orbits, pulling the cables rigid. Now each cable becomes two spokes with a connecting arc. The keel-weights (mostly) flatten the arc between the spokes, and all the cables, spaced equidistantly around the hub, provide the spokes for a great big wheel. Keep the whole thing rotating and you have a rigid framework for your LSM. With no stiff spars at all.

Now send spider-bots down the spokes and have them start stringing cables from spoke to spoke, start at the midpoint of each arc, and the weights as well, because you're going to use the tension to control the final shape. Connect everything with ribbon tape. Lay a roadbed. It's a suspension bridge without towers, everything joined at the center, turning round and round, and held in place by centrifugal force. Keep stringing cable and ribbon tape. Work your way up the spokes, connecting everything. Round and round all the little spiders go, crawling patiently around the circumference of the wheel, until they've woven a whole great web of wires, a gigantic whirling hoop. Now you start laying down your plastic wrap, unrolling it round and round and round just like the cables and the ribbon tape.

Okay, all that makes it sound a lot easier than it really is. Actually, you have to construct five concentric wheels simultaneously, each one nested inside the other, like little Russian dolls. You do that so you can have multiple levels of gravity, just like the whirligig; but also because that gives you the security of five bulkheads between you and vacuum.

And remember, you have to do it twice, because you need two LSMs. And a third one too—the "machine shop." But once you've got everything turning, once you've got your fabbers turning out cable and tape, the whole process is automatic. The spider-bots are patient and uncomplaining. They only come back in when they need another reel of cable and fresh power cells. As they run the webs, a second set of spider-bots installs hatches, monitors, sensors, electrical harnesses, fiber-optic cables, pipes for plumbing and ventilation, accessibility tubes, pneumatic delivery systems, dumbwaiters, elevators, all of the hidden systems necessary for maintenance and viability.

It sounds like a lot, but once you've got those big wheels turning, you can see how much there is and how little there is, both at the same time. With all the lights on, they look like grand empty outlines, amazing and awe-inspiring, every detail of the still-unbuilt wheels delineated like schematics brought to life, rotating proudly against the diamond stars. All the supports and cables, the spokes and interconnections, all the plumbing and wires, the lights and harnesses, everything connected together, rolling and turning, two of them, identical, rotating in opposite directions, but visibly syncing up every 10 degrees in a bright double vision that collapses into a momentary eclipse of brightness and then unfolding again like a kaleidoscope as they continue spinning past. A gigantic, flickering, headache-inducing, psychedelic display.

Of course as soon as we started, long distance stills and videos of our wheels started showing up all over the ecliptic. Anybody who had a scope pointed it at us. We were photoed from the super-Hubble, photoed from the ultra-Webb, photoed from the Kenya beanstalk, photoed from the 30-meter Lunar Darkside Observatory, photoed from the Phobos Base, photoed from sixteen different traction-drive vessels with near-space trajectories, photoed from around the arc of the belt—all those photos didn't give any sense at all of how beautiful our wheels were. Not until we published our own pictures. We put out a handful of drones to send back real-time views from edge-on, above, three-quarters, and flyby.

Of course, there was a lot of speculation about our wheels, what all the various harnesses and plumbing would eventually connect to, so along with our progress reports, we also posted our intended structural completion dates, certification target, and when we intended to start taking reservations for the first Asteroid Belt Tourist Hotel and Theme Park. Facilities would include picture window viewports, specialty suites with Lunar/Martian/Terran gravities, null-gee full-body shower-massages, asteroid mud baths, solar sunbathing, outings to the flying mountains, starsuit EVAs, bubble-ball, null-gee bridal suites, and anything else we could think of that you would want a luxury space hotel to provide. Most of it we cribbed from the brochure of the *Hotel Enterprise*, that big fake starship tethered to the beanstalk in low Earth orbit, but nobody seemed to notice. Unfortunately, unlike the *Hotel Enterprise*, we didn't have any simulation-rights, so none of our avatars could look like famous actors.

We also announced a contest for people to submit theme ideas for our hotel, the winner would receive a free two-week visit, all expenses paid, including transportation. That part was tricky, Ganny was afraid we could be sued for fraudulent advertising. But I said no, read the fine print. IRMA was very careful. If we didn't open a hotel, the contest was null and void, and we weren't really opening a hotel anyway, we were building a spaceship, remember? But it was fun imagining the hotel anyway. I started out wanting a Stanley Kubrick motif, but after a hundred or so almost identical contest entries, I decided it was overworked and actually a little creepy. Ganny favored a Jules Verne theme for a while. That would have been fun, but the more we played with the design of our lounge, all that varnished wood and dark red padding started to look heavy and wasteful and ultimately oppressive. Ganny and I both agreed that we wanted something that looked light and bright and playful, but at the same time homey. And easy to maintain.

We both wanted light, lots of it, all different colors, warm and cool, depending on the season and the moods of the people in the room. Lots of green plants, flowers, fish, e-candles, fountains, glowing mist-bowls that doubled as humidifiers, sheer hanging curtains to define spaces, and even a few overhead fans, the old-fashioned kind that were operated by turbaned slaves pulling braided cords, only instead of slaves we'd use theme-bots to pull the cords.

We were so engrossed in planning our fictitious hotel we barely acknowledged the red team when they left. There wasn't that much for them to do anymore and the bots were handling 90% of it anyway. So the team had been keeping pretty much to themselves, just running out the clock. I hadn't seen Grillo, the team leader, for a couple weeks, it was almost like he was avoiding me. The few I did see were very formal and polite, nobody called me short-stuff anymore. Nobody even mock-flirted. If I had cared, I would have minded, would have felt hurt, but I'd already started distancing myself from them when they asked for cash up front, so I just grunted in response to anything they needed to tell me.

Even so, we planned the traditional shift-change party for them, even though we weren't changing shifts, we were shutting down, so the party had a funereal edge to it. But Ganny wasn't going to let her emotions show. She put out her best spread, all the traditional meats, ham and turkey and roast beef, all the best fruits and vegetables and cheeses too. It puzzled me, because I thought she was in a "good riddance to bad rubbish" mood, but then I realized what she was doing. She wanted to give them a good case of the regrets. Wherever they went, they'd end up comparing the vittles to Ganny's best and coming up short. And not so obvious, she wanted the red team to go on to all their wherevers and tell everybody that if we were hurting, we sure weren't showing it.

Even so, after they left, the gig felt kind of empty. Hollow. Even lonely. And we still had to finish shutting down the last of the traffic, diverting most of it to Spinward and the remainder to Anderson-Base. We were only taking contracts that specifically required the orbital advantages of the Whirligig, either catching or tossing—and we charged premium prices for the effort, because Ganny just didn't want to be bothered. Every catch required a human being watching over the systems, a finger poised over the abort button. I'd done it, but only with Ganny or Gampy standing by. One week before my eighteenth birthday, the Big Gig was essentially out of business. We still got the occasional buy-out offer, but most of those were speculators making half-hearted inquiries. Equity sharks looking for a quick turnaround.

Meanwhile we were focusing on the next step of construction—how to wrap the wheels, how to panel the decks and the bulkheads. The problem wasn't that we didn't have a good way to do it, the problem was that we had too many good ways. We were looking for the sweet-spot, what would work best and what we could afford and what we could accomplish quickly. There's an old saying in engineering: "Good, fast, cheap. Pick two." We were trying for all three.

Actually, all that planning, all that designing, all the discussions back and forth, a lot of it was hard, most of it was hard, but it was a lot of fun too, some of the best fun we'd ever had. Except some of it was bittersweet. Every so often, sometimes almost every shift, Ganny and I would just stop and look at each other and one of us would say something like, "Gampy should have been here to see this," or "Gampy would have laughed," or "Gampy would be so proud of this." And sometimes we smiled and sometimes we stopped and cried a little. And sometimes we just got wistful for a minute or two, until one or the other of us would say, "Okay, that's enough. Gampy wouldn't like us wasting time like this. Let's get back to work."

Now, about those decks and bulkheads. That's what made Ganny laugh the loudest. After all those many times she said she'd never sit down and knit, not for anyone, now she was knitting the biggest longest scarves that anyone in the whole ecliptic had ever knit. At least a couple dozen.

Well, actually she didn't do the knitting, the knitting machines did, back and forth, back and forth, shuttling way too fast to see what they were actually doing on each pass, but each time back and forth, back and forth, adding a new row of intricately looped fiber. Back and forth they went, hissing and buzzing, clicking and clacking. Back and forth, patiently rolling out huge rolls of material, endless rolls, great barrels of triple-knit weave that would ultimately become the floors and walls and ceilings of the wheels.

Okay, yes, the machines did the actual knitting, not Ganny—, but Ganny designed the system, so the knitting was hers, all hers, and as all the different cylinders of fabric began to stack up in the "machine shop," Ganny's grin grew broader and broader. "Yes, this is going to work. This is really going to work."

Let's say you're making cloth. The obvious way is to weave it over-under-over-under, the material is kinda like a checkerboard. But it's not the strongest fabric you can weave. If a single strand breaks, you've got a place where there's extra stress on surrounding strands and that's where the rip is most likely to start. No, it's a lot stronger to knit your fabric. Or even double-knit. Or triple-knit. Because you've got your thread all hooked around and through itself, in and out and under and over, to make an intricate fabric of multiple interlocked loops. If you knit nano-fiber, the result is an air-tight material so fine you can't even feel the weave. Well, it's not really air-tight, it's just that the knit is so tight that most large molecules have a real hard time squeezing through; we use that a lot for starsuits. And graphene too. If you knit micro-fiber, you get a soft silky fabric loose enough to breathe and wick away moisture and feeling really nice against your skin, great for underthings, and we can sell it as space-lingerie in our fictional hotel. If you knit standard carbon-fiber, you get a larger scale of knit, lightweight and very resistant, it doesn't wear out. And so on. All the way up to titanium cable, which gives you a very impressive chain mail. You can knit anything, whatever size yarn or wire you want. You could even knit elevator cables if you needed to, if you needed a net strong enough to catch an asteroid. Or an Enterprise fish. But probably not a giant space amoeba. If we ever met one, it would probably ooze through the mesh.

Ganny set the bots to work weaving all these different knits, because she needed at least six different scales of tensile strength: micro-strength for the smallest of assaults, macro-strength for major events on the hull. She had IRMA run all kinds of simulations, and eventually we decided to panel the wheels with lasagna—multiple layers of knit, each layer pumped full of honeyfoam.

Honeyfoam is a generic term for quick-hardening poly-crete. It creates a layered, bubbled substance; if you mix it right and spray it right, you get uniform-size bubbles and an internal structure like a honeycomb. Very strong. Each bubble stays liquid inside. If something punctures the foam, the liquid bubbles out and reseals the foam just as good as new. Plus honeyfoam also helps against cosmic rays and radiation.

A lot of dirtsiders think that metal plating is the best defense against little cosmic bullets, but it isn't. A cosmic bullet hits a molecule of metal and it splits off gamma radiation, which is even worse. Instead, we can dope the honeyfoam with particles of magnetized plastic and when the wheel spins, it creates a strong enough magnetic field to deflect a lot of radiation. Not that the stuff doesn't respond to magnetism, but if we can reduce the overall exposure to what Ganny calls "sea level on a cloudy day," we're okay. Flip the polarities on the second wheel, the one that spins in the opposite direction, and the two magnetic fields overlay and combine instead of cancelling each other out.

Anyway, we let all three wheels spin for a few weeks to make sure they were stable, no wobbles, nothing seriously off-balance, all the stresses and strains equalized across the frames, everything working, boards green, confidence high, viability optimum, 110 percent, five by five, lock and load, surrender Dorothy, and metaphors be with you. Everything.

One night, over dinner—it was Ganny's turn to cook and she was experimenting with breaded hamster nuggets, I don't know why, but they turned out better than I expected—Ganny put her fork down and said, "Starling, I want to tell you something."

The way she said it, I expected bad news.

But no. "When we started this, I didn't believe it would work. No, really. Let me finish. I honestly thought it was a crazy idea, but I figured if I could you get involved in the planning, it would distract you enough to let me focus on the really hard decisions. And also, I believed, you'll laugh at me now, but I believed that when you finally bumped your head up against the impossibility of this whole thing, you'd finally accept the inevitability of the tougher choices we would have to make. I never expected to get even this far, but I am so glad we did. Watching you grow into the job has been the most joyous experience since I don't know when. Gampy would have been so proud of you. I wish he could have seen how passionately you've thrown yourself into this job and what you've accomplished so far."

I started to push my noodles around on my plate, trying hard not to blush or cry or fall bawling into her arms. I wasn't used to Ganny being all maudlin like this. But Ganny reached over and pushed my chin up. "No, you. Let it in. All of it. You've done good. And even while all the math still says we're crazy, still says this won't work, still says we're dancing so far out beyond the skinny twigs we're way overdue for a splat—even though this has got to be the single stupidest idea since polarized milk, I want you to know, I am committed to seeing it through. I've burned our last bridge."

"Ganny?"

"Well, think about it kiddo. Once we launch, what happens to the Big Gig?"

"Um." I hadn't thought about it. "It'll still be here, won't it?"

"And where will we be?"

I started to answer, then I shut my mouth. We were going to be all over the ecliptic. I looked around at the galley as if I'd never seen it before. The gig was…my whole world. The benches, the fish, the canoe, the rose bushes, Gampy—

Ganny pointed out the window, at the big wheels spinning grandly only a few hundred meters away. The third wheel wasn't quite hidden behind them. "That's our new home, sweetheart."

I didn't know what to say. I looked at Ganny. I looked out the window again. I looked back at my plate. I wiped my nose. I rubbed my eyes.

"It really is real, isn't it?"

"That's what I'm trying to tell you. Yes." Very carefully, she began explaining. "We wouldn't be ready for at least eighteen months. Maybe two years. But we were going to need a crew. Six, maybe as many as ten. I've set up a dummy site, operating out of a Martian provider. It's a hiring service, referring crew to open berths, mostly in the belt. It's all automated, linking in to all the majors, but we get to look at all the best applications first. Anybody with a rating of 82 or higher. Shipmasters start filling their cards a year before launch. We need to start making bids if we want a qualified crew."

Ganny was right. I nodded thoughtful agreement. "I guess there's a lot I haven't thought about. I've been so busy focusing on the mechanics of construction, I haven't been thinking about…anything else." I felt like an idiot. I put my fork down. "You said something about burning a bridge?"

"The gig. Look, I don't want anyone to figure out what we're up to. They'll find some way to stop us. Maybe they'll try to decertify our hull before we launch. I don't know. I'm not going to take the risk. So everything we do, we have to make it look like something else. So I've changed my will. Just a little bit. It'll look like I'm only rearranging things because Gampy's gone, but it's really something else. I've sold an option to Spinward. It says that if for any reason I am no longer able to maintain operations on the gig, you take ownership. If you're not able to maintain operations, or if you choose to relinquish your rights, then Spinward Station can exercise their option."

"What if they don't want to?"

"Oh, they do. They've already in the process of transferring the full purchase price into an escrow account. They have 24 months to raise 50% of the capital, with a payment plan on the back end for the rest, plus points on all contracts for the first 75 years of operation. They think they're getting a bargain, they think they're doing me a favor, they think I'm planning for your future. And…they think my health might be a little bit more fragile than it really is."

"Ganny!"

"I didn't lie. I just told them my real age."

"You didn't."

"I did."

"You're shameless."

"I am."

Over ice cream, this time homemade peach, we started making plans for our new home. The wheels were not only bigger than the gig, they were wider as well. We would have nearly three times the floor space on each of the gravity levels. That meant we could have bigger farms, bigger lounges, bigger gardens, bigger everything. Even bigger koi ponds. We'd have to make a lot more topsoil. Even so, we'd be stripping a lot of the value from the gig.

"Can we transplant the rosebushes?"

"Already planning on it. And Gampy's bones too. We're not going anywhere without him."

"What about Spinward? Won't they feel cheated if we sail off with all the topsoil?"

"They don't want it, they're cleanliness fanatics. They prefer to grow plants aeroponically. But there's a clause in their contract that gives them rebates for any reduction in viability, anything that becomes unavailable due to your actions or mine. The contract does not include any part of our new construction." She nodded toward the window. "Or any of the materials used in that construction. I was very careful about that. They're only bidding on what's left of the gig if we leave, regardless of circumstances. Don't worry, they won't be disappointed. They want the bottom half, not the top. They want the industrial pods."

"Oh, okay."

A week later, we started carpeting. First, the plastic wrap. We made a big deal about that, not for ourselves, but for all the paranoid dirtsiders. We flooded the pipe with photographs and videos and animatics showing how the whole thing was supposed to work. We wanted them arguing whether or not it would work, arguing how ambitious and outrageous it was. We wanted them applauding our audaciousness while they morbidly speculated about how and when we would die and how horrible it would be and if we would be transmitting our last moments live. We wanted them to believe we were tiny and toony, and all a little loony. Ohell, we wanted them to think we were as flat-out crazy as a revival meeting.

We let them watch for weeks, while the bots trundled round and round the circumferences, laying down "road-beds," the bottom decks of the wheels, unrolling layer after layer of see-through plastic wrap, until we had a surface nearly a centimeter thick, much more than we really needed for this layer, but we wanted the dirtsiders to get bored. Really bored. By the time we started wrapping the spokes, our viewership had dropped to only the most fanatic members of our audience. The ones who believed we were secretly planning to drop asteroids on their heads.

Then one shift, two of our photo-drones inconveniently collided while maneuvering into new positions and went permanently offline. Coincidentally, the very next shift, a whole new set of bots began "laying carpet." Unfortunately, the only available close-ups of this aspect of construction were long shots from drones much farther out and at very inconvenient angles. It made it very hard for anyone offsite to get a good look at the way we made lasagna. Ganny apologized profusely and promised to fab new camera-units as soon as she could.

But that's when we got serious with all the stuff we didn't want anybody getting a good look at. Ganny didn't want people seeing what level of technology we could apply to the problem. What we had was graphene. Large sheets of it. Rolls of it. Lots and lots of it. Enough to wallpaper a planet.

Graphene is one of the strongest substances ever manufactured. It's another one of those things you can do when you convince carbon atoms to behave themselves and line up nice and orderly in one-atom-thick sheets. You could stretch a piece of it over the top of a coffee cup, suspend a pencil over it, put a three mega-kilo cargo pod on top of the pencil, and the graphene still wouldn't puncture. Roll it up tightly in tubes and you have cable strong enough for a beanstalk. Or a whirligig.

The best graphene is fabbed in a null-gee vacuum, shielded from intense solar energy, but even way out here in the belt, you still get microscopic flaws and cracks, so if you're going to make cables out of it, you have to interleave multiple sheets as you roll them up. We had a lot of graphene rolls, we fabbed it even when we didn't need it and sold it to anyone wanting to build a beanstalk or a whirligig or hang a tent over a crater.

In its sheet form, graphene is good for strengthening all kinds of things, and if you could mass produce flawless, uniform rolls of it, it would be one of the best construction materials in the universe. But so far, nobody has managed to produce more than a few dozen meters of flawless. So you have to wrap it in multiple sheets. Or in our case, just keep wrapping around and around and around. And around. The graphene foundation was necessary for what came next.

Now, we laid down layers of nano-knit and carbon-polyfiber-knit and all the others, and of course more graphene sheets too, balancing them for strength and flexibility. That's another thing dirtsiders don't understand about engineering big things. You have to allow for expansion and contraction, stretching and shrinking, crinkling and cracking, material fatigue and fabrication flaws, and then add a dollop of wiggle room for bouncing and bumping. So we balanced heavy-knit and tight-knit and sheets of pure graphene. We sprayed honeyfoam over and under and inbetween everything, and if anything ever stretched or flexed or cracked enough to break the foam, the foam would just fizz for a second, harden, and repair itself. And of course, we also laid down grids of monitors between the layers to measure temperature, radiation, proximity, vibration, movement, flex, stress, pressure, deformation, internal sound levels, impact, leakage, contamination, material decomposition, and the possible presence of ethereal heffalumps and other boojums. And anything else we could imagine. Because we were designing this ourselves, we were going ultra on the specs. And then as all the internal monitors became active and we certified them, we began growing the matrices for an IRMA installation. Our ship wasn't going anywhere without a brain.

Then for a long time, it felt as if nothing was happening. The big wheels kept on turning, the spider-bots kept unrolling. They pushed the cylinders of fabric rolled around and around the decks like prehistoric dung beetles pushing giant dinosaur turds. Other spiders manipulated huge cones, unwrapping great arcs of material around the spokes. Very quickly, the wheels stopped looking like outlines of themselves and started looking like…wheels. And whatever was happening inside, the view rarely changed from one day to the next. We knew that progress was happening, we just didn't feel it.

So we concentrated on other things. We started moving all the necessary support pods into place both above and below the wheels. Raw supplies, processed food, oxygen and nitrogen tanks, gas-scrubbers, fabbers, all kinds of raw material for the fabbers, maintenance and repair equipment, spare bots and replacement parts, anything and everything. We cleaned out the closets, the pantries, the garage, and the attic. Then we started moving the life-support systems, too. Aeroponics, hydroponics, meat farms, more oxygen and nitrogen tanks, more gas-scrubbers, more fabbers, solar storm bunkers, lifeboat pods, emergency life-support units, starsuits, rebreathers, hazmat suits, O-masks, airlocks, and more bots. Did I leave anything out? If I did Ganny would catch it. Whatever she missed IRMA caught. And of course, we had all the checklists too. We had a century and a half of modern shipbuilding to draw upon and all the associated recommendations, requirements, specifications, tech manuals and certification sheets. We were pumped.

Inside the third wheel, our engines were taking shape too. The wheel itself was going to be our radiation shield, protecting us from the emissions of our own drives. There wouldn't be much radiation and most of it would be directed aftward, but just the same, starside you minimize every risk, to yourself and to everyone you approach.

The bottom wheel was made of overlapping leaves, not linked at the sides and permanently connected only to the top rim of its hub. Just before launch, we'd release all the cable connections on the bottom rim and the wheel would unfold like a gigantic flower, opening out to become a great grand dish and revealing our engines to space. We'd keep it spinning for a few weeks while the spiders crawled across it, anchoring the separate petals along their edges, linking them together and forcing them into a gently curving concave shell. Then we'd spray them with heavy-honeyfoam, both inside and out, to give them permanent rigidity. During that whole time, we'd be running final tests on each of the engine tubes. When all that was finished we'd unroll the primary traction drives, big feathery things that would look like three gigantic oversized pistils sticking out of a very small flower. When everything was finally in place, the ship would look like a gigantic shuttlecock with a sharp pointy tip. We'd have the biggest traction engines ever built and 9 small secondary units spaced within.

If we could avoid any serious missteps, then eight weeks after launch we'll have tested and certified every major drive component. Allowing for the usual last minute unforeseen, unpredicted, and unexpected adjustments, calibrations, fixes, and repairs, the entire ship would be all-green in fourteen weeks. I would be nineteen and we would be starborne. We'd have not only the fastest ship in the system, we'd also have the most comfortable crew quarters.

But right now, we had to finish attaching, loading, and balancing the supply and equipment pods that clustered the length of the keel. And after that, we had to build and install the gear to make the habitat wheels viable. Neither wheel had yet been certified as spaceworthy, we hadn't even run preliminary pressurization tests, but if we started viability construction now we could minimize load-up time later.

Once all that was underway, we began to review applications. While we had been focusing on the hardware, the first few inquiries had already begun trickling in. Mostly desperate wannabes, but not all. A couple were interesting, we put them in the "definitely maybe" file.

We'd decided on a total complement of eight. The two of us, at least three more women, three men. We didn't need a full crew for the shakedown. And we could probably run with four if we had to. But Ganny wasn't saying everything she was thinking yet. I knew her moods well enough to recognize this one. I didn't say anything. I figured she was still working something out by herself, having one of those internal conversations with Gampy, and she'd let me know later if she decided it was worth pursuing. Then it would be my turn to chew it over. I suspected she was thinking about ship-families and teams and long-term relationships. She was thinking about me and my future.

This is another one of those starside things that dirtsiders don't get. "How do you live with the same people day after day, week after week, month after month?" But you could ask a dirtsider the same question. "Why do you get married? And live with the same person month after month, year after year?" Except they don't. As near as I can tell, dirtsider marriages are like mayfly mating seasons. Twenty-four hours long.

Starside, you live with people practically forever. Once you launch you're set for the entire journey, both out and back. So joining a crew isn't about taking on a job, it's about joining a family. Yes, you have to have all your tech-skills in place before your application can even be considered, but after that the real question is what can this person contribute to the family? Does he or she play any musical instruments? Play chess? Poker? Starcraft? Can he/she cook? Raise crops, tend a farm, manage a vegetable garden? Does this person have medical or dental skills? (Yes, I know. Every ship has medi-bots, but it's nice to have a human doctor too.) What fields of continuing education is this man or woman pursuing? What research is he/she currently engaged in? Does the candidate have an interesting personal history? A repertoire of interesting experiences to draw upon and share? Is he or she a good teacher? A coach? A trainer? A counselor? Does this person know when to shut up, when to withdraw? What do others have to say about working with this individual? Does the candidate use the ship's gymnasium? How often? How does this person feel about communal bathing? Does he/she practice nudity? How does this person manage his/her personal hygiene? What is his/her sexual orientation? Does he/she snore? And even though we're not supposed to consider it as a job qualification, it still is one—is this person attractive? Do you want to spend time with him or her?

And then…after all that, after you've accepted someone's application, you put in a confidential bid for their services and then they review *your* folder to see if they want to join *your* starside family. But the starside community is a small one and people have reputations, good or bad or mixed. After you've shipped a few times, you learn how to read folders, you learn what to look for. And what to *look out* for. Somebody who's served on a lot of ships might look good at first glance, but what if it's only one tour on each ship? What does that tell you? What if she's served seven years with one crew and then abruptly quit? What does that mean? What does all that psychometry tell you about ultimate compatibility?

The big problem was that neither Ganny nor I had a lot of experience in crew selection. That was usually the crew chief's responsibility, red or blue. Whoever we picked, we would be taking a big chance. There were a few people we knew, folks who had worked for us on the gig in the past, but the ones we would have invited were already booked for the next few years, and most of the ones who were available were people Ganny never wanted to see again. She didn't go into detail. If I had ever met any of them, I didn't remember. When you're little, you form your memories from a much smaller perspective.

Ganny was thinking that we needed to protect our secrecy right up to the last minute. Maybe we could have our prospective crewmembers train for our ship on simulators at Anderson Base. Anderson wouldn't even need to know who the sponsor was, we could run it through our Martian dummy company. Wheels within wheels within wheels. Literally.

And then—in the middle of all this—someone tried to kill us.

When traffic to the gig was at its very heaviest, we would catch and sling as many as a dozen pods in a four-hour shift. After the traction drive made it possible to build very big and very fast ships, slinging cargo into the pipeline was only cost-effective for the lowest priority cargos—things that would be needed soon or later or eventually, but weren't needed *now* —what the shippers called "futures" but we called "staples." Like extra supplies of air, water, emergency kits, scrubbers, rations, spare parts, fabber components, raw materials for fabbers, toilet paper, stuff like that.

By the time Gampy died we were down to six pods a day—on a busy day. When the red team left, we were doing half that. And after Ganny finished shutting down all but the most essential contracts, we were doing less than that in a week. And most of that was stuff that had been in transit for a while. Some of the owners had been able to course-correct their cargo-pods to Anderson or Spinward, but not all, so we still had traffic.

In past years, there had been a healthy "futures" market in pod-traffic. Speculators would load and launch a pod with all kinds of goodies, but with no specific buyer on the far end—in the expectation that by the time the pod arrived a year later, somebody would pay a premium price for a cargo that was already in the neighborhood. That was a nasty game for a while, with belters bidding against each other for premium cargo, until Gampy organized a co-op, and all of a sudden the auction market collapsed because almost nobody was bidding. Gampy caught over a dozen of those speculative "futures" pods that arrived at the Whirligig without a buyer. That's when the real fun started. He purchased the cargo at a dime on the dollar and resold it to the co-op at forty cents. Then the belters bought what they wanted for fifty percent of original value. That might have been one of the reasons the dirtsiders hadn't liked Gampy very much—because he was better at their game than they were.

But now—there were no more pods. In only a few years, the market had evaporated. A lot of investors took big losses. And the gig ended up overstocked with everything the buyers had abandoned. There was no longer a futures market, and if we saw more than a few pods a week, we experienced it as an annoyance, not a duty, because it pulled us away from the much more interesting challenges of ship construction. But our rule was that we always had to have a human finger on the abort button. No matter what.

Which was why Ganny and I were both on deck when the assassin pod came in. We were trying to figure out an alternate cargo cluster configuration on the keel of the ship, and at the same time fussing over what to make for dessert tonight. We were almost to the point where Ganny was going to win one argument and I was going to win the other when IRMA buzzed—loudly. The pod was coming in fast and its orientation had shifted. Ganny didn't even have to flip the plastic cover off the abort button, IRMA popped it for her. Half a second later, every alarm went off, the pod was firing its course-correction thrusters. It was aiming for the hub of the whirligig—the central control core—us. Hitting us at speed, it would shatter the keel of the gig.

The gig is big—a huge spinning disc—but it's not unbreakable. Imagine a spiderweb twenty kilometers across, with additional strands going out another ten, twenty, or thirty klicks, each with a ballast pod at the end. Or even a much heavier ballast rock on the major spokes. The combined mass is considerable, the torque of the spin even more so. It's pretty much an immovable object, a spinning immovable object. Just below the web, or above, depending on your orientation is the spinning doughnut of the living modules and control core. Cargo pods were supposed to link up with the outer ring of the web, or occasionally even the hooks at the end of the ballast rocks, depending on the approach velocity. But this cargo pod suddenly pointed itself at the keel of the gig and accelerated inward, a self-firing cannonball. We had less than three seconds to impact—

Of course, it never hit. It got caught by the Gulliver nets. Essentially invisible, a network of wires and beanstalk-cables, strung from all over the keel of the gig to thousands of points all over the spiderweb disc of the wheel, hundreds of thousands of strands, covering every degree and each one studded with hooks. They work like arresting cables. Individually, none of them are strong enough to catch a pod, but collectively they're damn near impenetrable to the kind of traffic we get. If a pod comes in wrong, too narrow, too close, it will get caught by the turning wires. We might end up breaking a lot of cables in the process—they're fabbed with different strengths, all the way from a little brittle up to extremely elastic, so if they're hit the breakage is staggered sideways and around—and the contents of the pod are swung into place over a period of several seconds instead of instantaneously. It makes for a more survivable catch, both for the contents and for any passengers who might be riding as cargo.

The assassin pod caught, lurched, swung, almost hung, then caromed sideways and exploded. Most of the shrapnel missed us. One of the empty storage pods in the junkyard took a hit, but it wasn't a pressurized pod and the damage was easily repairable. Less than an hour's work for the bots. We didn't feel even a thump. Neither Ganny nor I said anything for the first few seconds. Not even a curse. Finally, she very quietly pushed the plastic cover back onto the abort button, leaned back in her chair and calmly said, "IRMA, track that bastard back to its point of origin."

Of course, it was untraceable. The pod had been slung to us from a whirligig at one of the Martian LaGrange points. The launch came from a dummy company, contracted by a dummy company, hired by a dummy company, licensed through a dummy company, owned by a dummy company, in cooperation with a dummy company, so many levels deep that even Ganny was impressed. The chain of responsibility was not only old and cold, but most of the links had already been removed. Somebody wanted us dead and we didn't know who. Or why.

The motivation could have been anything from a long-delayed and now-useless revenge against Gampy's co-op to a preemptive strike against the launch of our spaceship—the latter was far more likely. And if so, then somebody dangerous had put a lot of pieces together. Not too hard to do once you figure out that Ganny is both committed and capable. When you understand the circumstances, then you also understand the author of the circumstances—and that defines your options and your choices. Somebody was looking over our shoulder. Somebody was copying our homework.

Ganny thought about all the possible responses we could make, then opened a private diplomatic channel and sent this message: "The next time someone tries to kill us, we're going to start throwing rocks. We have a target list. You can guess what's on it. Maybe Mecca, the Vatican, Jerusalem, Moscow, Washington DC, Beijing, Dubai, New Delhi, Paris, Disney World, Clavius, Tranquility, Turtledome, Burroughs, Asimov Station, or even the Beanstalk Terminus in Ecuador. Or maybe some other sites we aren't mentioning. If we do it, we'll sling them around the sun so they come up out of the glare, impossible to see until it's too late. It doesn't matter who authorized the attacks on us, we'll retaliate on the most convenient targets, and you guys can sort it out among yourselves who deserves the blame. Or if you're really smart, you'll figure it out among yourselves *now* so that there are no more attacks. And in case you think I'm bluffing, remember those pods we dropped into the Pacific all those years ago? Dropping them into the Pacific was a courtesy. We're through being courteous." She closed the channel, looked at me, and said, "That should do it."

"I'm not sure I understand—"

"It's politics, honey. It's not about playing the game, it's about playing the players. It doesn't matter if we know who did it. *They do.* Or they know how to find out. They'll very politely tell the folks who tried to kill us to knock it off. Or maybe not so politely, I don't care. They're probably not worried about our threat, they know how to track and destroy a rogue pod long before it becomes a threat. They learned how to do that after Gampy taught them the necessity. But just the same, they can't take the chance that we'll fling a heavy load of gravel at them, or something else they can't stop as easily. So they'll spread the word around: *Hands off the crazy lady*. And if somebody tries something again, they'll retaliate on our behalf and we won't have to. It's like playing Assassination Poker, only with real bullets."

We never got an official response to Ganny's message, but we got several unofficial notes. Nobody said anything specific. Mostly it was polite sympathy at our narrow escape, praise for having such effective safety mechanisms (that they had never known were actually in place), several unconvincing promises that the ultimate ownership of the death-pod would be thoroughly investigated, and only a few vague acknowledgments of anything beyond that—except for one obfuscatory letter suggesting that if somebody was out to kill us, their next attempts would probably not be so obvious. Like we needed to be told that.

Ganny looked at me, I looked at her. She said, "You know what Gampy would say right now?"

"What?"

She scratched her neck gently with the backs of her fingernails. She put on her deepest voice and a thick Italian accent: *"But I didn't know until this day that it was Barzini all along."* To my puzzled expression, she said, "Okay, movie night tonight. My pick. I can't believe we left out such an important part of your education. There's an important lesson you need to learn—oh, and for dessert we'll have cannoli. I'll teach you how."

A couple of weeks after that, almost enough time to start feeling normal again, Ganny got a confidential email relayed through a Lunar proxy. "I am writing on behalf of a private information resource entity. We do focused data-mining in various technological and engineering domains. From time to time, we discover confluences of significant interest. Where we feel it is appropriate, we volunteer our services as agents, negotiating contacts of mutual benefit between entities who might otherwise would never have come in contact. Because we recognize the critical value of personal privacy as well as corporate privacy any information that we gather is treated as extremely confidential. We never release or exchange private information without first paying for the privilege of doing so.

"Recently we have become aware of an entity looking to charter an interplanetary vessel capable of high-speed, high-capacity delivery of cargo and passengers to multiple destinations within the populated ring of worlds, moons, colonies, asteroids, whirligigs, and space habitats. Attached is the list of projected specifications and requirements for cargo and passengers.

"We are writing to you because of your reputation, your experience with long-term starside habitation, and because you are uniquely situated to have knowledge of trustworthy independent contractors willing to work outside mainstream channels. All of our data-projections suggest that you represent a very useful avenue of inquiry. We recognize the unorthodoxy of contacting you this way, but we believe the circumstances warrant it. Our data maps suggest that the possibility of significant mutual benefit is very high. If you are intrigued by this possibility, we would establish confidential and secure procedures to put you in contact with the above-mentioned entity. Even if this is not an opportunity that presently suits you, we still hope to establish a relationship with you for the development of other opportunities in the future. Please reply to this confidential address if you wish to continue this discussion."

Ganny read it aloud, then passed me the e-page to look over. "What do you think?"

I shrugged. "Somebody knows."

She nodded. "Somebody who wants to hire a smuggler. And they think they're being very coy about it."

"Not smuggling," I said. "Freelancing. And not coy. Careful."

"Is that what they call it now?"

"Ganny, this is the free market in action. There's no regulation, no enforcement, and a lot of money to be made."

"Starling! I had no idea you were a libertarian. I thought we kept you away from that antiquated foolishness."

"Ganny! Don't be silly. I'm not a libertarian. I'm a greedy capitalist. Big difference. Real capitalists don't whine. There's a lot of money to be made in freelancing. That's what you and Gampy always wanted to do."

"What we wanted was to give you the career you've been training for all your life."

"I know. So we should talk about that. Where do we want to go? What do we want to do?"

"It probably won't be a long conversation. You've been crunching numbers for six months. I've been waiting for you to tell me what we're doing."

"I thought you'd already figured it out. Saturn."

Ganny raised an eyebrow. "Saturn?"

"We don't have enough gas to fill the wheels. We can only pressurize them to fifteen kilometers. Even if we enrich the O-mix, even if we wear O-masks, we're still going to have side effects—like pre-packed meals, because we can't do any real cooking where water boils at room temperature. We can't steal gas from the gig, that's not fair to Spinward, it violates our deal with them, and it isn't practical to crack gas from an asteroid because that's another year or more sitting around waiting before we can launch. And we lose our window to go collect our stolen goods. So instead, we live in the pods for a couple weeks while we ship out to Saturn, collect ice from the rings, crack it for gas, fill both centrifuges and pressurize them to sea level. Isn't it obvious? And while we're out there, we grab as big a berg as we can and bring it back. Enough to fill the new lake at Luna City—it'll be cheaper than lifting the same mass up from Earth and we can show a profit on our very first trip."

"We might get a better price at Asimov. And it's a lot closer."

"Mars? But that's where MEBC is located and—" Oh. I got it. A dish best served cold. Ice cold. "Okay, that works for me too." Sure. Let's knock the bottom out of their private little water market. That would be a very nice gift to the Martian farmers. "We'll need an agent to resell the water—?"

"Already handled, not a problem." Ganny didn't have to explain. The biggest monopoly on Mars is water-cracking. It's not impossible, it's just slow, tedious, and more expensive than you'd think. Plus you have to pipe it from where the water is to where you want it. In principle, it's easy. In practice, it's a bitch requiring a big investment in heavy equipment. If you have the heavy equipment, it's a seller's market. But if you don't, well then Mars isn't heaven. They've got you by the short and curlies, if you're one of those people who still have short and curlies. If not, they've still got you. Selling cheap water to Martians could overturn the planet's economy. Ohell, if we had a fleet, we could overturn the whole system. Hmm, a fleet....

Ganny must have been reading my mind again. She added, "We've also got agents on Luna and here in the belt. Dark agents. No one knows it's us yet."

"Some people suspect," I said. I'd looked at a couple of the deep data-mining sites, where folks speculate on all kinds of things, in this case, the very slight uptick in employment offers without a corresponding uptick in scheduled ship launchings. And various other contract inquiries. "But, Ganny—I don't want to be a truck driver. Saturn is only a shakedown cruise. I want to do something else."

"I know. I've seen how you've outfitted this ship. You want to go for the long ride."

"I'm that transparent?"

"You're that transparent."

"Well, I sort of figured we'd do like we planned from the beginning. We'd pick up our pods, the ones we can get to, allow our unfaithful customers to renegotiate for delivery, or maybe we just take back our stolen stuff and keep it, but either way we finish up as much old business as we can, maybe take another year or maybe two running around the ecliptic, testing ourselves, sorting out our crew, getting settled in, and then…when we're sure we're ready…we grab a load of colonists and head out to…y'know, where none have gone before."

Ganny nodded thoughtfully, taking it all in. "Well, at least you're giving yourself time to think about it. It is a long ride, sweetheart. You'd better be sure. You'll be years away from everyone else." She paused to wipe something from the corner of her eye.

"But you're coming with, aren't you?"

"I haven't decided that part yet. The long ride is a journey for younglings."

"You're still young—"

"Physically, yes. Emotionally…I feel as old as time. Maybe I'd feel different if I still had Gampy." She reached across and patted my hand. "But we don't have to decide that now. Let's take this one shift at a time." She took the forgotten e-page from me and held it aloft. "So, what do we tell this wannabe smuggler?"

83

"Nothing. It could be a ruse. Like Jimmy Sawyer."

"Ignore it?" She was ready to shake the page blank.

"Um. No. Let's find out what he knows about us. Ask him for more specifics. Don't say why."

The reply came back three days later. It was not what we expected. Ganny's face was ashen as she passed the plastic sheet to me. The bad news was the video. A whole column of video windows down the right side of the page. The entire construction of our ship. The top window showed the keel being moved into place and attached to the bottom of the whirligig's axis. The second showed the bots stringing the first cables. The third showed the hubs spinning and the cables sailing out to form a wheel shape. The next showed the completed frame and the spider-bots layering the first rolls of plastic wrap. The last showed close-ups of the bots rolling out the first layers of knit. Whoever it was—they knew everything. We had no secrets.

I looked at her, confused. "Someone tapped our private channels?"

"No. Look at the camera angles. We never put any drones on that side of the junkyard. Someone got smart. They must have attached a device to the outside of a cargo pod, probably a pod of supplies or equipment that we ordered for our own use, something we'd pull in instead of slingshotting it off somewhere else."

"But we haven't pulled in any pods since—oh, frack."

Ganny figured it out the same time I did. The drone had been attached to the transfer pod that the Red Team arrived in. Either with or without their knowledge. Probably with. As soon as it could detach without being slung off, it must have released and taken up position less than a klick off our axis.

Frack, frack, frack. And double-frack. It wasn't Jimmy who'd told. Now, I felt really stupid. I'd made an assumption. I'd fragged him. I'd shut him out. I'd slagged him with nastiness. I couldn't even apologize. I'd probably hurt him so bad he'd probably given up and gone for the mind-wipe. Googol-frack.

"I wonder how much those bastards made betraying us," Ganny said. Her expression was as dark as I'd ever seen it. "That explains everything. I wonder how many other spybots they planted." She was too angry to waste time cussing, she was already rising from her desk. "We're going to have to sweep—"

"Wait, Ganny—"

She stopped.

"Did you read the text?"

Her hands were trembling. Badly. She reached for the page. As she tried to focus, I said, "I don't think they're trying to blackmail us."

She started reading slowly. "Thank you for your quick response. You will likely see the attached videos as an intrusion into your privacy and for that we sincerely apologize, but we believe the need for contact is urgent. Let me explain.

"Several years ago, we determined that various stations in the asteroid belt would be good candidates for independent surveillance. The attached files confirm that judgment. While you have publicly stated that you intend to build a space-hotel, much of your construction also appears to be well-suited for the assembly of a long-range vehicle. We presume you have already considered that possibility. If the addition of traction drives are indeed a part of your future plans then we have several opportunities we would like to present to you.

"Additionally your construction methods could also have system-wide applications and we would like to discuss this with you as well. We are in an excellent position to explore, extend, and maximize your technology. Recognizing the critical time-factors involved, we want to arrange a personal meeting as quickly as possible. We have an agent who is familiar with your circumstances and can leave immediately. If you agree, we can have our agent at your station within two weeks.

"Please be assured that we recognize the critical importance of protecting your privacy. Even within our own organization, access to the attached files and the details of your construction methods has been severely restricted. Regardless of the outcome of our discussions, we will protect your technological secrets. I hope to hear from you soon. Sincerely, etc."

Neither Ganny nor I recognized the name at the bottom. A quick goggle provided only three lines of information. This company was a dummy for someone or something else. Just like Ganny's Martian and Lunar dummies. Did everybody distrust everybody so much that they only did business through sock puppies now?

We talked it over, we walked it around the centrifuge, we sat on Gampy's bench and tried to figure out what he would say. We thought about it privately. We went to bed without making a decision. We slept on it. We woke up in the morning and had waffles. We finally decided to send back a single sentence. "We're thinking it over."

Six hours later, the reply came back. "We'll pay for the meeting. A thousand liters of sea-level oxygen. A thousand liters of sea-level nitrogen. Two thousand liters of water. Five thousand seed packets. A thousand protein cultures."

"They're rich," I said.

"They're desperate," Ganny replied.

"They're afraid we'll launch without them."

"I wish I had their faith in our abilities. We're still a month away from lighting up the new IRMA."

"It's only a meeting," I said.

She shook her head. "I'm not sure I want to trust a stranger on the gig, not this close to launch."

"One person. Bring him or her in through the security lock, deep-scan down to the bone, and surround him with armed-bots?"

"Maybe."

"We could use the seeds. And the water. And especially the gas." I added, "It's enough to get us to Saturn."

"They did their math. They're smart."

"We have something they need. Maybe they have something we need…? I think we should listen."

So Ganny wrote back. "And ten gallons of Double Double Chocolate Fudge Swirl ice cream."

They replied. "You drive a hard bargain, lady!"

"Hmp," said Ganny to me, not to them. "I'm no lady."

"They'll find that out soon enough."

Six hours later: "Our agent is on the way."

Ganny turned to me abruptly. "All right, that's settled. Now tell me what you're so mopey about."

"Does it show?"

"It shows."

"Jimmy Sawyer."

"I thought you didn't like him."

"I don't. But I owe him an apology."

"So write him."

"I did. But he's gone."

"You searched?"

"I can't find him anywhere. He's disappeared. It's like he doesn't exist anymore." I finally said it aloud. "I think he went and got wiped. And it's my fault."

"It's not your fault, sweetheart. Everybody is responsible for their own decisions. If he did, then he did what he did because *he* chose to do it. You're halfway across the solar system. All you did was send him an email."

"But it was a bad email!"

"Whatever he did—it's not your fault."

"But it still feels like it."

"Yes, that's the part that hurts."

Ganny hugged me and I cried into her shoulder. And that helped a little. But not as much as I'd hoped. This was something I was going to be ashamed of forever. Gampy used to say, "Being stupid is no disgrace. Staying stupid is. Clean up your messes and move on." But how do you clean up a mess that can't be cleaned up? Jimmy was the only dirtsider I'd ever really liked.

Ganny whispered in my ear. "The pain doesn't go away, Starling. You just learn how to live with it. And that's the hardest part of growing up. Walking around with all that pain that just won't go away." I guessed that was what I saw in grownup eyes, the part I didn't like. I didn't want to look like that, but now I knew I did. There wasn't enough frack in the universe to express how I felt. So I cried into Ganny's shoulder until I couldn't cry anymore. And then I went to my cabin and crawled into bed and wrapped myself up in my favorite soft blanket and just felt bad about everything until I finally fell asleep.

When I woke up, everything was in uproar. Ganny had asked IRMA if we had to, how soon could we launch? IRMA said 23 days. That's how soon the engines could be brought on line and tested. Almost all the rest of the construction could be finished in transit. And the stuff that had to be done now, so we could launch—IRMA compiled a list. So Ganny activated every bot and put them to work. Even the new cat. She activated every processor in the local cloud and commandeered everything with a clock cycle. IRMA coordinated schedules and there was an e-page and a sandwich stuck to my door. All I had to do was take things in order and check them off as fast as I could get to them.

A lot of it was simple manual labor. Grab this, carry it here, install it there, bring it online, let IRMA test it, certify it and sign off. Some of it was supervisorial. Double-check the certification of all the sub-units. Eyeball the pod-load. Send in a probe, walk it by remote, look through its eyes, listen through its ears. When you're satisfied, put on a starsuit and walk both wheels, all five levels—the three habitat levels and the two storage spaces, five different gravities. This time, *feel* the environment. Motion sensors will tell you that it doesn't wobble, doesn't tremble, and that the pseudo-gravity is stable. Walk it anyway. Feel it. I didn't see Ganny until dinner time and she looked as frazzled as I felt. But I didn't have to ask why.

If one somebody had figured out what we were up to, then it was possible—almost inevitable—that a lot of somebodies had figured it out, too. And if it was someone who didn't want us to launch, we could have bad news on a collision trajectory. Oops, I'm sorry. Your spaceship accidentally got in the way of our missile test.

After dinner, Ganny said, "Okay, here's the part I did without checking with you. You can get mad at me later." She opened a schematic on the big display. She didn't say anything. She just let me study it.

"Hm," I said. I pointed. "Rail-guns. Needlers. Laser-cannons. Missile launchers. Particle beams. Silent screams. Pain projectors. Funny-foam. Tanglefoot fields. Spider-nets. Stunners. Disruptors. Isn't this a little overkill for pirates? Are we going to topple a government? Or are we just going to war against the Klingons?"

"Yes," she said.

I wasn't kidding about the Klingons. There's a whole colony of them on Luna—fanatics who've gone from cosplay to full-sim to body-mods and the more extreme are even going for genetic modification. Most of them don't have much to do with humans anymore and the feeling is apparently likewise. Dirtside intelligence engines have already projected open hostilities when the third generation hits maturity, sometime in the next twenty years—with the Klingons losing badly and having to go into psychometric rehabilitation. But that's another discussion. Personally, I find the wannabe Vulcans a lot more annoying. Kind of like objectivists, but passive-aggressive. I don't understand any of that stuff. Why pretend you're from a fictitious planet when there are real planets just a few mega-klicks away?

Ganny said, "We've had a pretty large arsenal for a long time, punkin. We've only needed it once, but that once was justified. We've kept most of the defensive gear hidden in the core of the junkyard, the rest is very well disguised and scattered in the most unlikely places. Spinward doesn't know about this stuff, at least I don't think they do, and I'm not leaving it behind for them. So as long as we're schlepping it, we're going to make it cost-effective."

"Ganny, *this* is a warship. Just pulling into orbit will look like a threat to some folks."

"As long as we don't *look* like a warship. As long as we don't make noises like a warship. As long as we pretend we're not, they'll pretend too. Because it's convenient not to have large crowds of people running around in a panic. You know your history. Remember? The big dog sent its ships sailing into ports all over the marble with nuclear weapons in their bellies, but nobody talked about it, nobody got publicly upset, but everybody knew, at least the ones who most needed to know. And the big dog stayed the big dog until it got so flea-ridden it bled to death. The little dogs feasted on its bones and the ones who got too big inherited the biggest fleas. That's life on the marble. And they're trying to export it starside."

"But—if we install all these weapons, aren't we behaving the same way? Just as paranoid as they?"

"Absa-tootley," she agreed. "There's the paradox. You want to leave any of this stuff behind?"

"Hell, no. But I think you might want to mount the heavier weapons closer to the center of gravity to take some of the stress off the keel."

"Already considered that. It reduces our coverage. And the gear isn't mounted to the keel, it's mounted to a framework that clamps around the keel. It actually adds to the longitudinal strength. Oh, and I'll want you in the fire-control simulator at least an hour a day from now until launch."

That was a lot to think about. I knew Ganny didn't want to be the big dog. Hell, she didn't even want to be in the same pack with most of the other mutts. But maybe, like everything else, there was a lot more to this. My first thought was that Ganny wanted us armed against—against whoever it was coming to meet us. The "fast ship" they were sending might very well be a cruiser.

But the unknown guys in black hats who might be a bigger threat, the ones who might not want us freelancing—maybe that's who the heavy armaments were for.

But there was a third possibility too. It didn't seem likely, but there was a lot that didn't seem likely until it looked absolutely inevitable afterward. I had a lot to think about. And not a lot of time for thinking. I goggled what I could and skimmed it whenever I could grab a spare half-minute—in the toilet, on an enforced rest-break, or even while shoving a sandwich into my face.

Two hours before the fast ship was scheduled to arrive, I finally spoke up. "Ganny? Whatever he offers…we can't accept it."

"Eh?"

"If he knows we've built a ship, then he's gotta be smart enough to know we've armed it."

"Yep."

"So he wants to hire us as muscle."

"That is a possibility, yes."

"Ganny, he's bringing a Corporate Letter of Marque. It's the only thing that makes sense. Hiring us as independent agents to do somebody else's dirty work. We'd be privateers—pirates!"

"Arrrgh," said Ganny. "And it isn't even the nineteenth of Septemberrr yet."

"Ganny!"

"Starling, what do you think they're going to call us when we start taking back our cargo pods?"

"We have the Martian court's judgment."

"The Earth courts didn't recognize it." She put her hand on mine. "We haven't said yes. We only promised to listen."

"I wish we'd never built the damn ship."

"You don't mean that."

"Yes, I do. No, I don't. I just didn't realize—"

"You didn't realize, did you, that when you bring a really nice toy to the playground, you end up surrounded by a lot of other kids who want to play with it too. And if you don't share it, some of them will try to take it away."

"Ganny, I didn't grow up dirtside. I've never seen a playground, remember?"

"Yes, and I'm sorry about that. There are a lot of lessons you've missed."

"Foof!" I made one of those noises that I make when only a noise will express what I'm feeling.

She put her hands flat on the table. "Don't be too quick to make judgments. Sometimes, the pirates are the heroes."

"I'm sorry, I don't understand that."

"That's my fault. I neglected that part of your education. Look, the Martians might applaud our audacity at stealing back our own pods, but now we're talking about delivering cheap ice to Martian farmers. The farmers might call us heroes, yes. But what do you think the Martian ice-cracking companies are going to call us? Not heroes. Carpetbaggers. Wildcatters. Poachers. Privateers. Probably even pirates—because we're stealing their market. So who's the good guy? Who's the bad guy?"

"We are. We're the good guys."

"That's not what they'll say."

"Well, then they're wrong—"

Ganny patted my hand again. She did that a lot these days. "Sweetheart, it depends on where you stand. Not all pirates are…bad guys."

The way she said it, her tone of voice, the look in her eyes—I suddenly got it. All those things she'd never explained. All that history. "You and Gampy—?"

"Uh-huh. Me and Gampy. All over the backside of Luna."

"Oh." It took a moment to sink in. "Oh!"

"That's right. We started at Turtledome and—never mind. There'll be plenty of time later on to tell you the rest. You'll be surprised."

I looked at her as if I'd never seen her before. Cap'n Ganny, scourge of the spaceways. Amazing.

"You never told me."

"You didn't need to know. You weren't ready to know."

"I guess not." My head was spinning as fast as the gig. I was having trouble wrapping my mind around this. This was going to take some time to get used to. Maybe it was all a matter of definitions. Words. Attitude. Context. Where you were standing. I finally stammered, "So you think piracy might be a good career move?" It must have sounded stupid.

But Ganny answered matter-of-factly. "If we like the targets. If there's enough money in it. *And* if we're on the right side of the argument."

I thought about it. Yeah. This was what we'd been planning all along. We just hadn't called it what it was. No, I hadn't. I exhaled loudly. I nodded. "Okay. But only as long as we're on the *right* side of the argument."

"Agreed."

"Hey! Can we wear space-pirate costumes?"

"You can. I doubt I'd look good in a titanium bra."

"Ganny!" I gave her the look, at least as well as I could manage it. "You've been living in micro-gee since you were 18. You're a long way from Cooper's Droop."

"It's not the perkiness of the puppies I'm concerned with, sweetheart. You'll still look better in pirate drag."

"Arrrgh," I said. "You'rrre the Cap'n. Can I wearrr an eyepatch? Can I have a parrrot?"

"And a wooden peg-leg, if you want. But you might have to be a boy. There aren't many girl pirates. It's not the best career option."

"I'll be the captain of my carrrreer."

"You sure? You might like being a boy."

"Uh-uh." I dropped the rolling Rs. "I don't want one of those dangly things. I don't even want to *think* like someone with a dangly thing. Yick." Ganny and Gampy had always said that even a short time as a boy would be good for me, but I never could see the point in it. And I didn't want to have the "try it, you might like it," conversation again. Time to change the subject. "So, um, what are we going to name our ship? We need something dramatic. Something to strike fear in the hearts of robber-barons everywhere. The *Crimson Dagger*? The *Banshee*? The *Screaming Yellow Harpy*?"

"Nothing."

"Huh?" I was confused. "But I have a whole list—"

Ganny shook her head adamantly. "Put your list away. A spaceship names herself. When you get intimate with her, when she trusts you, when it's time, she whispers her name to you. Even a ship with a brave heart won't even know her true name until she's earned it. We'll have to wait to find out who she is."

"I never heard that before. It's not on any of the sites I've visited—"

"There are a lot of traditions we don't write down. You'll learn." The clock chimed the hour. Ganny glanced at it, looked back to me. "There it is. It's time. Get to your fire-control station. Remember how we trained. You stay locked on target until I give you the all-clear, nobody else. Even if the ship is docked. I'd rather blow away half the gig than surrender all of it. You understand?"

"Aye, aye, Cap'n." I even saluted.

"Good girl. Now, go."

I bounced.

I was right about the "fast ship" being a cruiser. Like all traction drive ships it had an oversized array of "feathers" sticking out the back. Not as big as what we would eventually have, but big enough to push this little dumpling around the system at a steady one-gee acceleration. We'd been watching it long-range for several days, but we couldn't get a good visual. It was painted black. With Sol a few degrees off its stern, we couldn't see much more than its silhouette in front of the coronal cloud. But IRMA enhanced the view, so we had a pretty good idea what kind of armament it carried. This thing was coming in fast. Maybe furious. We wouldn't know until it was too late.

She wasn't decelerating. That was ominous. If she were on an attack run, she'd want to drop her fish as fast as possible to minimize her own vulnerability. But if she were going to fire missiles or a beam, she wouldn't need to come in close. She could have launched them an hour away. But if someone were going to attack us, they wouldn't have to send a cruiser, they could have launched from Luna or Mars. Unless they wanted to launch away from witnesses. But even if they did that, the trajectory of the missile or the path of the beam could be traced, and it wouldn't be too hard for a skilled data-miner to determine what ships could have been passing through the locus of possible launch spaces.

There weren't so many ships in the system that the ship watchers couldn't keep track of them. They knew the orbit of every man-made object in the system, they knew what it was and where it was. The only objects they couldn't identify or locate—were dark objects, things built and launched in secret. But if you dug into the databases, apparently they knew where most of those were too. But possibly not all. This was not reassuring.

Then the signal came in and I relaxed. A little. She wasn't decelerating. She was aiming to catch a hook on one of the whirligig's rotating cables.

That was a sign of…I guess, trust. If we changed our minds, if we didn't want them docking here, we didn't have to catch them. But Ganny approved the connection and I watched my scopes as they began adjusting their trajectory to make the linkup. They had to match the speed of the line. They would have only a three-second window to catch the hook on the end as it came swinging up. If they missed it, or if the hook failed to latch, they'd keep on heading past while the cable swung away.

But they caught. Their hook caught our loop. Our hook caught theirs. The ship was already oriented nose in, so it showed only the slightest lurch when it was caught by the line and the centripetal force yanked it into opposition. Almost immediately, the gig began adjusting its balance, reeling out several of the opposing ballast pods, retracting the complementary ones. The service-bots were already attaching docking cables. Even before they were secured, IRMA was scanning the vessel. Top-to-bottom, a full-spectrum deep scan.

The layers of the schematic began appearing immediately on my displays. I had a pretty good idea what to look for, I didn't see anything alarming, but I wasn't an expert. IRMA labeled everything she could identify and extrapolated what she couldn't. Nothing unexpected. More important, all weapon systems were inactive and cold. But that didn't mean anything. A military-class weapons-package could be brought online in seconds.

Eventually, Ganny signaled green, and the docking cables began spooling up, reeling the ship in toward the center of the gig like a giant black fish. My job was to stay in place, a backup for Ganny. Watch and wait. The visitor's ship, curiously unnamed, connected to a docking pod opposite Level 2. Martian gravity. The two airlocks connected and equalized pressure, temperature, and gas mix. Neither they nor we were too far off standard, the process completed in 90 seconds. I readied my finger on the button. Whoever or whatever was coming through, there was still a chance he could come through armed. I didn't expect it, it wouldn't make sense, but that was precisely the reason for caution—that it didn't make sense.

The airlock hatch slid open. IRMA began scanning immediately. There was no one there. Only a refrigeration unit. Ten gallons of Double Double Chocolate Fudge Swirl. Nice. Ganny gestured and a cargo-bot rolled up, secured the unit, and wheeled it off to the galley. Very nice.

"Okay," said Ganny. "That's a good start. Where's the rest?"

The airlock door slid shut.

Just beneath the Martian deck, there was a cargo lock. Ganny and I both watched our screens. They opened their hatch, we sent a team of cargo-bots in. The seed packets were in a dozen cold-boxes, not big, I could have carried one under each arm. The protein cultures were a lot heavier. When the cruiser docked, IRMA had balanced its mass by rearranging cargo-pods, pulling some in, letting some out. But this was a balancing problem on a much more delicate scale. Now she had to pump water around the 'fuge to compensate for the shifting mass of cargo we were bringing aboard. The hibernation boxes with the protein cultures were heavy enough to warrant the concern. Plus, we had to scan them. We routinely scanned everything that came aboard the gig, but this time we deep-scanned each container from three angles and IRMA constructed an interior schematic of each for intrinsic analysis. There were no problems, but we didn't expect any. If these people, whoever they were, wanted to hurt us, they wouldn't do it this way. And if they wanted us to trust them, they wouldn't play games with the payment.

The gas and water we simply pumped aboard, but that took time too. IRMA had to balance all of it to separate ballast tanks. Ultimately, she'd move most of it down to the new wheels. But she wouldn't do that while the strange ship was docked, she wouldn't risk having the visitors monitor our operations any more than necessary.

It took over an hour to complete the transfer of cargo. When Ganny was satisfied that payment was complete, she went back to the lounge to meet our guest.

This time, when the airlock hatch slid open, there was a man inside. I couldn't see his face. He raised his hands and turned around slowly while IRMA scanned him. I was too busy studying the body-schematics to care what he looked like. He was lean. He was young. He was unarmed.

Ganny stood off to one side, where she was out of his field of vision. "Take off your jacket, please. Leave it in the lock. Your collar buttons are microphones. Your pocket buttons are cameras. And that look doesn't work for you anyway. You can keep your pants on, but remove your shoes please."

The stranger dropped his coat to the deck and pulled off the lightweight moccasins he wore. He waited until Ganny gave him the okay, then stepped out of the airlock. The hatch slid shut behind him. I resumed breathing and snapped the safety cover back onto the fire-button. By the time I finished securing, the stranger had already moved into the lounge. He had his back to the camera, he was silhouetted by the light, but the look on Ganny's face suggested something awful had just happened. I reached for the 8-second replay, but before I could hit it, Ganny said, in a very flat voice, "Starling, please come down to the lounge."

My heart sank. Ganny wouldn't have called me down like that unless—unless something happened we were both totally unprepared for. Had Ganny just surrendered?

"Starling?"

"On my way," I replied. I bounced out of my seat, swam down the access tube to the fuge, oriented myself appropriately and floated down to Level 1. Hit the stairs to Level 2 where real Martian gravity started to kick in and slowed down. Straightened my shirt. Ganny didn't know about the needle-beam strapped to my forearm—

I stopped at the bottom step. Standing next to Ganny was a tall, broad-shouldered man. He had a folder in his hands and he was smiling at me. He had ruddy skin, freckles, buck teeth, big nose, bright red hair, and he looked an awful lot like—

"*Jimmy?!*"

"Starling!"

"You're not dead—?"

"Neither are you." He grinned. He was older. Two years older than the last picture I had of him. He had filled out. He had shoulders, a chest, a haircut. He looked like a man now.

I took a half-step toward him, my body wanted to leap across the intervening space and hug him forever, but I stopped myself, hesitant, confused, still distrusting. The questions poured out of me. "I thought you were—I tried to find you, I couldn't. How did you get here? What the hell is going on? Ganny, did you know about this?" And finally, "Jimmy—" And that's when I stopped. My knees buckled and I sank to the deck. Slowly. In 0.38 gee.

Ganny crossed to me and grabbed me under the arms before I finished settling. She pulled me back up to my feet and whispered softly to me, so Jimmy couldn't hear. "Starling, sweetheart. First get rid of the needler strapped to your arm. I don't think you're going to need it and it's pulling your bra sideways. I'll teach you later how to conceal a weapon. Here, give it to me." She stood between us, keeping him out my view and me out of his; she reached efficiently up my sleeve, peeled away the gun and made it disappear into the folds of her jacket. She straightened me up, held me until she was sure I wouldn't fall down again, then walked me over to a couch. Like the majority of our furniture it was mostly foam sprayed on a plastic-wrapped frame, with a nice knit cover.

She pointed Jimmy to the couch opposite. "I think you have a lot of explaining to do, young man." She sat down next to me.

"It's not that hard to explain," Jimmy said, settling himself. He put his folder on the table. A bot rolled up with a pitcher of water and three glasses. "We were going to lose the rest of my college allotment anyway, so I sold it on the futures market. I mean, I know it was silly, but the money was going to disappear no matter, so what else could I do with it? It's against the law to harvest future dollars, you have to reinvest them. So I bought a probe. Ordered it through a proxy. Sent it out from a Martian company with your Red Team. I didn't mean any harm. I just wanted to take a photo of Starling waving at me, and I'd transmit back a photo of me waving back."

He paused. "Okay, that's not entirely true. All those long conversations we had—" He looked across at me. "It wasn't a hypothetical. You were designing something real."

"What gave it away?"

"You kept insisting it was a thought experiment. I believed you the first time. But the more you said it, the more I wondered why you needed to keep saying it."

"Oh," I said.

Ganny poked me. "Remind me to teach you how to lie. You're not very good at it."

"I guess not."

Jimmy spoke up. "I told you I wanted to come out to the gig. When I saw you were building a spaceship, I was all the more determined. When I got your message, the angry one, I knew I had to get out here, somehow. To apologize. To make it right, somehow."

"Apologize? But you didn't—"

"Hush, child." Ganny patted my knee. "If a man wants to apologize, let him. It doesn't happen very often."

"Look—" He spread his hands wide. "When we first started trading messages, I thought you were a fake, just another online joker pretending to be a starsider. There are a lot of those. I didn't even think you were a girl, just some old fat guy trolling for attention. Because you were too smart, too literate, too everything. I'm not the only one who thought that, either. Nobody else on the forums knew if you were real. We had a whole private discussion group. I mean, we liked you, you seemed honest enough, nobody ever caught you in a lie, but why would a starsider want to pay any attention to us? We heard starsiders were all self-righteous, arrogant, elitist snobs who wouldn't talk to groundlings, so it didn't make sense that you were really who you claimed to be. So I just led you along for a long time, asking you questions, drawing you out, trying to trip you up. But then you started sharing stuff you couldn't possibly have known unless you were real. I mean, anybody who wants to know about the Big Gig or Spinward Station or Anderson Base or any other station can goggle or wiki them. You can search for blueprints, crew rosters, supply schedules, virtual tours, economic analyses, annual reports, news articles—and of course, all the conspiracy sites too. But you knew stuff that wasn't on any of the sites. You knew the Red Team and the Blue Team. You knew everybody's nicknames. You knew personal histories. You knew everything. And the way you wrote about—it wasn't like you were making stuff up or reporting from a distance, you were writing it as if you were living it, so if you were a phony, then you were the best ever. *Or you were real.* But no sock puppy would ever go to that much trouble to fool a skinny geeky nerd-boy like me. I looked you up, but there was hardly anything about you. Just your age, who your parents were, how they died—I felt real bad reading that part—but not a lot else. Some school records. And a picture or two of you with the Blue Team, when you were small. You had the biggest eyes. You still do. But, I mean, your messages could have come from anybody pretending to be you. Except…there was that other thing. I researched the tracking records on your messages. When they were sent, when they arrived, how they were routed. A phony might have proxied his messages, bouncing them off Mars with appropriate time-lags, but your messages bounced in from everywhere, whatever was the shortest path, but…I mean, after a while, I just had to believe in you. I just had to. And then when I got your message…I realized you thought I was the phony. I am sooo sorry." He looked across at me with an expression of such desperate hope I had to put my hands over my mouth to keep from laughing. It wasn't funny, but it was. Like one of those old screwball comedies Gampy used to love so much where everybody thinks everybody is somebody else, not who they really are, and everyone is running around in circles like a big game of crazy-bot, because they're all tripped up in their own wrong assumptions.

Jimmy must have thought I was angry. With my eyes wide, with my hands covering the bottom half of my face, I must have looked appalled. "Starling? Please? I came all this way just for you."

I didn't know what to say. It was too much. Ganny spoke for me. "But, James—Jimmy—how did you get here? Who is this mysterious company that sent you?"

"Um." He stopped. He looked embarrassed. "Promise you won't get angry?"

Ganny looked at him sternly. "Y'know, when someone says that to me, I just know that what comes next is going to be very bad news." She took a long deep breath. "I'll tell you what I will promise. I promise I won't kill you."

She squeezed my hand. Hard. Until I said, "Okay. I promise I won't kill you either. At least, not quickly. And certainly not painlessly."

"Um." Jimmy swallowed hard. I could hear the gulping sound. It would have been funny, if what he said next wasn't so…so *wrong*.

"Okay. Um. I was approached. My company was approached—"

"You have a company—?"

"Um, yeah. Kind of. It doesn't do anything really. It's only a dummy. But everybody has dummies. It's how they move their money around. I started a whole bunch when I was thirteen. Because I figured someday I'd be rich and I wanted to be ready."

"So you're rich now?"

"I wish." He looked embarrassed. "But, see, I did all my inquiries and everything through one of the dummies. See, whatever you do, if you do it through a dummy company, then you're kinda protected because if somebody tries to sue you, they can't—they can only sue the dummy, and it doesn't matter if they win or not, because it's only a dummy, there's nothing there to collect."

"Yes," said Ganny, absolutely deadpan. "We know how that works." She gave me a sideways look. *Gampy and I mastered that trick seventy years ago.*

"Um. Yes. Anyway, my company was approached. They asked me if I did research, I said yes, they asked what kind, I said data-mining. Shipping. How cargo moved. Stuff like that. They asked me if I'd take on a special project. I said why me? They said that their data-mining division reported that I was doing the data-mining that they needed. That didn't make sense to me. But after we all finished dancing politely around the subject for a few cycles, they said that I was in a unique position to do the kind of research they wanted done. Um. They said they wanted to know what you were *really* doing out here."

He held up a hand quickly. "I didn't tell them what I suspected. I didn't say anything at all. Because I didn't know who they were. I mean, not at first. But I figured it out later."

Ganny wanted to interrupt, wanted him to get to the point. So did I. But neither of us spoke. Watching Jimmy fumble his way through his narrative was like watching a ballet dancer being both elegant and clumsy at the same time. I perched on the edge of the couch, leaning forward, elbows on knees, chin parked firmly between my hands, eyes wide, fascinated, astonished, enchanted. Ganny confined herself to an impatient get-on-with-it wave.

"They said they were studying the belters. Even tracking email. But they said it was a matter of global security. They said they were looking for comet-tossers who might throw something at a planet. The intelligence engines would flag any messages that had certain keywords. I mean, that was how they located you. And then me. And after they argued with themselves for a bit, that's what they said, they contacted me because they thought I might be useful to them. Because you and I, we had a—a relationship. Sort of. A friendship. A long-distance thing. They said that it wasn't just useful, it might even be profitable. They said all the right things. They were really very good. But, um, oh, see here's the thing. I never met any of them in person. It was all email, but I got the feeling that they were—well, it wasn't that they were hostile, but they weren't respectful. Not toward you. I mean, not like I thought they should be. So I began to, y'know, think that they might not be friendlies. And that whatever I might say to them, they would want to use it against you. That's when I started to think what could I do to help you. Because I just didn't want you to be hurt. I just couldn't stand it if something I did ended up hurting you. And then they said they'd pay my way out here, so I could look around, take pictures—" He waved his hand vaguely in the direction of the airlock. "They wanted me to spy on you!" His voice cracked nervously. "I couldn't do that—I just couldn't. But it was the only way I could get here. Honest."

"Who?" demanded Ganny quietly. Coldly.

His voice dropped to almost a whisper. "*They never said, but I figured it out anyway…. Martian Electric.*" He fumbled with his hands as if trying to mold the words into shape. "It was the time-lags of their messages. I figured it out the same way I figured out yours. And because of a lot of our messages to each other—about your thought experiment—were relayed through the Martian links, that was kind of obvious. To me, anyway. I mean, I only look stupid. People underestimate me sometimes."

"You don't look stupid—" I blurted, but Ganny put her hand on top of mine and I shut up.

"The Martians…." Ganny shook her head. She made a face. She said a word. "It's *always* the Martians. The goddamn Martians. What is it with those people? Do they have to own everything?" She sighed, more in exhaustion than exasperation. "It wasn't a very big secret, Jimmy. We already knew it was the goddamn Martians. But—" She leaned forward intensely. "The whole point of this interrogation was to find out if we could trust *you.*"

"Please," he said intensely. "You *can.* I thought I just proved that."

"Actually, you proved just the opposite," Ganny said, all the time squeezing my hand tight to keep me from speaking. "You just told me you're willing to betray your employer—that you'll accept money under false pretenses just to get what you want. If Martian Electric can't trust you, how can I?"

His face went ashen. He deflated. He looked like someone had suddenly sucked two liters of air out of his lungs. He sagged where he sat.

"What I mean is…" Ganny raised one legendary eyebrow. "Why shouldn't we just stuff you out the airlock and then go eat your ice cream?"

Poor Jimmy. For half an instant, he looked like he wanted to cry. But instead, he gathered himself up, he stuck out his jaw, he put on his game face. "Because," he said. *"You need me."*

"We do? Why?"

"Because. I know what the Martians are planning. You don't."

Ganny scratched her head.

"It better be good."

He cleared his throat, he looked around both ways, he lowered his voice. "Don't eat the ice cream."

"Really?"

"Really." He nodded grimly.

"Those bastards," I said. "Ten gallons of Double Double Chocolate Fudge Swirl. *Those bastards.*"

"Don't worry, honey. They'll pay."

Jimmy said, "I'm very angry at them." After a beat he added, "Because I paid for that ice cream."

"You did?" That was me.

"Uh-huh." He nodded eagerly. "And all the other stuff too. The gas, the water, the seeds, the ice cream. The Martians wouldn't pay for it. They said they'd pay for ticket, but they refused to pay for the cargo. I told them you wouldn't talk to anyone unless there was an advantage in it for you. They said if I wanted to buy my way in, I'd have to do it on my money, not theirs. So...I used the last of my credit, all my dummies. Everything. I spent ten years building it up, lending the same three hundred real dollars back and forth from one company to another, back and forth, back and forth, until they looked like half a million plastic dollars. On paper anyway. And I spent it all on you. Hoping you wouldn't make me walk home."

"Jimmy—" I interrupted. "I know how much that cargo is worth. That's more than a half million dollars. The gas, that's nothing. But the seeds and the protein cultures—"

"I did the math too. You didn't have enough air and water to fill your ship. But you only need enough gas to get to Saturn to pick up some ice. After that, it's not an issue. But if you're going out on the long ride, then you need the seeds and the protein cultures—"

Ganny and I looked at each other. Startled. Ganny nodded an acknowledgment. "Yep. He definitely is not as stupid as he looks."

"But...how did you pay for it?"

He hung his head for a moment, swallowed hard, looked up again. "I had to indenture myself to buy it. I'm contracted for the next seven years."

"You didn't! Jimmy—" I dropped my hands to my lap. "You did that for me?"

"Yeah, I did. I guess I'm what you would call a big stupid hopeless romantic jerk. Because I didn't even know if you felt the same way, I could only do what I thought you would want a boy friend to do for you."

Ganny leaned over and whispered in my ear. "He is definitely a keeper. If you're not going to take him, I will."

"Ganny!"

"I'm just letting you know—"

"Um, excuse me?"

We both turned back to Jimmy.

"There's more," he said. "I do have…a business proposition. I mean, I knew you were building a spaceship. You did a pretty good job of hiding it, but I had one advantage nobody else did. I knew Starling. I know how she thinks. A little bit anyway. I mean, all those conversations have to count for something."

He leaned forward intensely. "Starling, remember how you said a spaceship is just a big can of gas. It only has to hold air and move, the rest is details. So if you've already got a life-support system, all you need is an engine. Remember when they added engines to it, how they turned that space station into an interplanetary craft? They sent it back and forth to Luna, then to Mars and back, even to Jupiter once, and what's left of it is still shuttling cargo to the L4 point. And after the Martians cancelled your order and you announced a hotel in the middle of nowhere that nobody would ever want to come to, it wasn't too hard to figure out what you were really planning. You've got all those drive engines you use for pushing asteroids around. I didn't see them when we came in. The Captain scanned you, of course. You've already got them installed, haven't you? I was afraid I wouldn't get here in time, that you'd launch without me. Without hearing me out."

He reached for a glass of water, but before he could drink, Ganny reached across and took it from him. "Not that one." To the bot, she said, "Klaatu barada nikto." The bot rolled away and another one came back with a fresh pitcher and three new glasses. Jimmy looked from the water to Ganny and back to the water.

"It's all right, go ahead."

He took a careful sip. "Um, okay. There are some people. Not the Martians. *Other* people. They're looking for a ship. A big ship. A fast ship."

"And you told them you had one."

"No." He shook his head. "Of course not."

"You told them you knew someone who had a ship."

"No." He took another drink, bigger this time. "I told them I wanted to get out to the belt."

"That's it?"

"I told them I might know some people who knew how to build ships. Who could build them a ship. A big ship. A fast ship. Away from prying eyes. That got their attention. I told them I was probably one of the few people who could even get in the door. They said they were willing to listen."

"Arrrgh," I said, quietly. Ganny poked me in the rrribs. Harrrd.

Jimmy shook his head. "I don't think so."

"Tell me it's not Klingons."

"It's not Klingons," he said.

"Who?"

"So, you're interested?"

Ganny and I looked at each other. Ganny spoke first. "If they have enough money to send us *twenty* gallons of Double Double Chocolate Fudge Swirl, they might have enough money to rent our attention."

"Invisible Luna," he said.

Ganny snorted. "Invisible Luna doesn't exist anymore."

"Yes, that's what they want you to believe." The joke wasn't funny. He spread his hands. "I mean, that's how invisible they really are."

Ganny rolled her eyes. "Listen to me, sonny boy. Gampy and I were part of Invisible Luna. Seventy years ago. The *real* Invisible Luna."

"Yes, I know. That's why these people will trust you. They don't like the Martians any more than you do."

"Hmpf," said Ganny.

I said, "We have some obligations we want to take care of first."

"I assumed that would be the case." He put the glass of water back down on the tray. "The people I represent—sort of represent—the other entity I want to put you in touch with, they want to see a sample of your work. So that's what I came to ask. Could we arrange a flyby? Or a visit to a neutral port?"

Ganny and I looked at each other again. *We?*

"Um, yeah. That's the other part of my…um, plan. I want to join your crew." He looked embarrassed. "If you'll have me. If you'll buy my indenture."

"Hooo…." I said. A noise, not a word. Totally involuntary. I meant it one way, he probably heard it the other.

Ganny put her hand on my leg—to stop me from making any more noises. "We'll talk it over."

Jimmy nodded nervously. "My ride leaves in six hours. Whether I'm on it or not."

Ganny said, "We'll talk it over *quickly*."

"How much is the indenture?" I asked.

He picked up his folder off the table and passed it across to me. "It's all in here."

"Who owns the indenture?" Ganny asked.

"The Martians," he admitted, embarrassed. "They've already put it up for auction. There are bidders."

Ganny's smile had a cold edge to it. "So if we don't buy it—?"

"—I'm screwed. And you're a lot richer."

Ganny took the folder from me. "Jimmy, the fact that you've made a series of impetuous and foolish decisions, all based on a hopelessly romantic assumption—perhaps even a delusion—does not obligate us in any way to rescue you. This is a business for us. And our lives."

"I know," he gulped apologetically. "But…." He looked at me, hopeful. Then he shrugged and surrendered to his fate.

"All right," said Ganny. "We'll talk it over." Something in her tone of voice. The conversation was closed. She stood up. So did I.

Jimmy realized he was being dismissed, so he stood up too. "May I wait here for your answer?"

Ganny nodded, an "if you wish" kind of nod, then led me spinward to an unused cabin. She opened the folder, studied at the terms of his indenture contract. "Not too stupid," she said. "Y'know…we could purchase this indenture through six levels of dummy companies. One of our Lunar shells could do it. Put a small down payment against a larger payout on the back end. And then…after reselling the indenture to another dummy, it goes bankrupt and defaults, dissolves without assets. It'd be another nice way to screw the Martians. And we end up with an already paid-for hired hand." She pulled a keyboard over, started tapping, losing herself in the process for a moment. "Yeah, we could do it. We've got a couple shells that we've been deliberately taking losses on, just for a possibility like this. And I do like the part about screwing the goddamn Martians. Okay, the mechanics are doable." She typed a moment longer, setting up the channels, then turned to me. "What do *you* want, munchkin?"

"I don't know—"

"Kiddo, you're the one who's going to have to live with him. He's a love-struck puppy. So was Gampy. He chased me till I caught him. So that's the question here. Do you want to catch this one? Or are you throwing him back?"

"He's awfully presumptuous."

"So are you."

"I am?"

"Yes, you are. But I love you anyway." Her voice became softer and more serious at the same time. "Just tell me what you want and I'll make it happen." She rattled the folder. "This indenture is expensive, but he's already paid for it in cargo, so it evens out. Or it would, if we were going to buy it with real dollars. Screwing the Martians is a bonus. But I expect they're expecting it. And if they are, then we're going to have to dodge another pod, real soon. Or something. But—" She put a hand on my shoulder. "—it looks like Jimmy's loyalty is unquestionable, sweetheart.

And he's smart, awfully smart. He didn't get out here by accident. He can pull his weight. And we do need crew. So we can make this work. *If you want it.* But you'll have to decide fast. I have a lot of juggling to do here."

I thought about how I would feel if Jimmy got back on the black ship and we whirled it back to Earth or wherever, what it would be like, how I would feel. It wouldn't be like the past fourteen months of me being angry at him and then another few months of being angry at myself. And then even more months of feeling bad because I couldn't make it up to him. This would be worse. This would be knowing I'd maybe had a chance and thrown it away. I'd end up wondering about all the might-have-beens.

So I knew all the reasons I wanted to say yes. I missed talking to him. I missed sharing things with him. I missed wondering what he would look like without any clothes on. Well, no, I could still do that. I'd been doing that for a long time.

But I also knew all of the reasons why this could be a colossal mistake. I didn't really know Jimmy as a *meatspace* person, had never spent any one-to-one time with him, didn't know if we really matched at all. I'd never even held his hand! What if this was a lot more wishful thinking than practicality? What if five weeks from now I realized how much I really hated him, his mannerisms, his quirks, his idiosyncrasies, his bad habits, that funny little hair that stuck out of his left ear, and just wanted to shove him out the nearest airlock? What then? I'd still be stuck with him, wouldn't I?

How was I supposed to make a decision about the rest of my life with no time at all to think about it? My belly hurt. Other parts of me tingled. Not all of it was unpleasant.

"Ganny, I don't know. What should I do?"

"What does your heart tell you?"

"It's not my heart. It's my gut."

"Starling. Darling Starling. You know what's right. You do."

I lowered my eyes. I studied my feet. I shook my head. I didn't know if my heart could tell me anything anymore. I swallowed hard. I caught my breath. This was going to be hard. Very hard. Maybe the hardest thing I ever had to do in my whole life. But it had to be done. *Now.* "Okay," I said. "I'll tell him."

Ganny followed me back to the lounge. Jimmy stood up as we walked in. I crossed directly to him, wrapped myself around him and planted a great big kiss on his face. For a first kiss, it was pretty clumsy. So was the second. But we got it right the third time.

45685084R00071

Made in the USA
Middletown, DE
19 May 2019